HATRED FOR BUGS

VICTORIA LORIA

Published by Victoria Loria Rawrt LLC
victorialoriarawrt.com

ISBN: 979-8-9988979-0-0 (paperback)
ISBN: 979-8-9988979-1-7 (e-book)

Edited by Leilani Dewindt

Cover art by Emiliano Figueroa

Printed in the United States of America

This work is fiction. All characters, organizations, and events portrayed in this novel are either
products of the author's imagination or are used fictitiously.

Thank you, Mark, my love, for making all this possible.

You are the perfect example of a loving, sexy, admirable man.

CHAPTER 1

I feel something crawling on me, tickling my skin. Maybe, just maybe, it's a piece of hair that fell from my crown. Only, it's not. Instantly, I'm filled with dread. The feeling of goosebumps forcing my arm hair into the upward position makes me look down at the eight-legged creature. Terrified, I release a loud yelp, flinging that thing into the air like clockwork. My heart sinks down into my chest as I look to the side to see Lucas, the bug, with an evil smirk. I run to the restroom, *again*, infuriated. The nerve of this guy. Ridiculous. My hand feels numb being run in the freezing cold water.

"Aguanta un pocito más Mija," is what my grandma would say in this situation. To keep pushing forward and holding on a bit longer. With only a little more customer information to be inputted into the file, the day will be over, and I can cry in peace. Letting him see my tears will only make the situation worse as he feeds off my pain.

Lucas immediately starts to rant when he sees me take a seat. "Now you've done it. Take a look at the computer and tell me what you did."

I look at the screen to find that during that whole scene with the spider, I accidentally clicked submit with the work unfinished. There was only one more paragraph left to go. Now I'll have to take the blame for something that was not even truly my fault. Even if I were to tell the bosses what actually happened, they probably wouldn't believe me. I hate him. More than anything or anyone in this world. Why does Lucas have to exist?

"Oh no, I see what I've done wrong. I can fix this."

"I'll have to report this to the bosses. Don't worry, you can stay late on Monday as well to fix what you've done. Now pack everything up. We're going home."

"Wait, please. I can't get in trouble again. I can't lose this job. I can easily fix it, and it won't take..." I beg.

"Upupa, be quiet. Not another word. You are going to have to pay for the mistake you've made. There is no time left to fix it. If we stay any later, we'll both be in trouble for staying overtime. You and I both know the bosses like to save their money."

I can't hold it any longer. Cold tears come flooding down my cheeks. Not another word escapes from my lips. What's the point? With this man, my breath is wasted. This has been going on all my life. Lucas and I have known each other since kindergarten. The teacher sat us next to each other. Being the shy girl that I was, I tried not to bother anyone. Lucas made me even more uncomfortable as he stared at me often. The rest is history.

Friday is my most hated day of the work week since the "manager" always finds ways to make me stay late. This morning, I contemplated staying in again, but my low bank account and bills coming due wouldn't allow for it. Getting my little car repossessed a few months ago doesn't help the situation either. Oh, how I wish I could walk out of this place right now for good—never to return.

The two of us have never been friends, more like pure enemies. I landed this job as an office administrator after making the decision to stay away from going to college. Student debt wasn't an option I could handle straight out of high school. The goal was to work my way up to becoming a financial advisor. I spent hours on hours making this facility a better place for customers and fellow employees. The bosses even teased me that if I kept working hard, I'd get a promotion in no time. That is until Lucas wooed the HR manager into hiring him onto my team.

Working hard is not a problem for me since my parents taught me to always take accountability for the things I do with my hands. From a young age, my parents expected me to be able to cook, do my homework without being told, and clean up after myself. All my teachers had very high expectations. Being a Cuban American put a ton of pressure to be the best at the time. Being an only child, my parents wanted me to be a doctor.

My entire life, Lucas did everything in his power to make sure I was the most hated kid in school. He initiated the terror. My hair would be pulled during recess, and red ants would be placed inside the back of my shirt. I'd scream for help like a little girl being kidnapped, which made it appealing to all the sick bullies.

Teachers and principals saw the constant injustice but did nothing except tell me to stop "messing around." My dad tried to teach me that bugs were more scared of us than we were of them by taking his shoes and socks off to squish them. It was very sickening to hear the crunch and see guts all over his bare foot. Disgusting. I hate bugs just as much as I abhor that man, Lucas. In fact, he *is* a bug.

It's still pouring rain. Man, I need to get away from here. Far, far away. I can't listen to another word from that evil man's mouth. If I lose my job, I'll never get my car back from the repossession team. My credit is going to be destroyed. The chances of ever getting a house for my parents will be annihilated. What about my life? What's going to happen?

CHAPTER 2

I plop down on my old couch that I bought from a college graduate as my phone yells at me annoyingly to check my notifications. There are three missed calls from Mom. She knows my Friday situation.

"Hi, Mom, another bad day." I sigh. "What advice do you have?"

"Have you thought about what I mentioned the other day?" She gets straight to the point. I've told her hundreds of times that ruining their retirement is not part of the plan. Moving back home would get me nowhere.

Though she'd never admit it, I know she doesn't actually want that. When I lived there for eighteen years, they couldn't wait for me to move out so they could get back to the way their lives used to be. Before I was born, my parents traveled together quite often. They would go to Cuba every six months to visit family and offer many gifts. Being a Cuban immigrant meant providing for family members who lacked a lot of the things we were blessed with here in the U.S. They would also travel to different states just to pick up souvenirs. During a trip to Key West, as they gazed towards the ocean next to the ninety-mile to Cuba sign, my mom informed my father that she was pregnant. He was very shocked but took it well. Even now, I can tell they had me way too young. In our culture, it was normal to have children right after getting married without even having a career or proper plans in place financially.

"Listen, Ma, I know you mean well. But I really can't. I've been thinking about, well, traveling. I've been dreaming about it for years. I don't have the money, so it might be a while until I can accomplish doing so."

"Really? Well, why didn't you say so?"

"Huh, what do you mean?"

"I've been waiting to tell you this until you were ready." She took a deep breath. "Your father and I have been saving funds for you since you were a baby, just in case you wanted to go to college."

My ears must be deceiving me. No one ever mentioned a college fund before.

"Mom, are you kidding me? Can we talk about this more in person? I'll come over first thing on Sunday morning."

"Oh, sure, but make sure you come before church. Let's attend as a family."

"Of course, Ma. I love you. Night."

MY EYES FORCE themselves open when someone comes banging on my door loudly as if it's an emergency. What sick person would disturb me right now when I barely got enough sleep? *Oh no.* Maybe it's the landlord demanding my payment that's been overdue for a month. I don't have enough to pay the full amount. Not even close. The schedule for getting paid at my job is once per month on irregular days. If I budget everything correctly and stay home on the majority of weekends for the rest of the year, I'll be able to pay him back in no time. The truth is the money is hidden in my savings account as an emergency fund, just in case I've had enough and can't take another day of the cruel bug, Lucas. I look through the peephole to prepare a perfect excuse, but to my relief, it's only Sarah who stands there, looking extremely concerned.

"My goodness, Sarah, you almost gave me a heart attack," I say, opening the door and pulling her in.

"Why? Were you expecting someone else? Or are you involved in some kind of crime?" She laughs.

"Of course not! Crazy. So, what's up?"

I can't imagine ever confessing to Sarah about the missed payment that's quietly lurking in my savings account. My loved ones tend to weigh every possible outcome, scrutinizing the pros and cons before making any significant decisions. They'd disapprove of my actions. But I feel stuck. Asking for help is out of the question. My friends and family are already dealing with their own financial issues, even though they constantly remind me that they are here for me. It hurts too much to take any kind of money from others. More of that pain is admitting that I've made bad decisions.

"I just wanted to stop by to make sure you're okay but also to invite you to go to South Beach. So, get ready because we're leaving right now."

"Whoa, whoa, whoa, hold on a minute. Who said I wanted to come? Also, it's like eight o'clock in the morning. You know I barely get any sleep these days."

"Actually, it's one in the afternoon. Are you really okay? I'm seriously worried."

"Oh. Sorry, I was tossing and turning most of the night, especially with these weird dreams. I was scared to look at the time."

"Did something happen at work last night?"

"Yes, I messed up the paperwork that I stayed late to input.

That creep Lucas found a random spider and placed it on my hand."

"Wow, he would do that." She sighs.

I smack my hand on my forehead. "Yeah, I don't know if the bosses will give me another warning or if they'll just let me go."

"If you want, I can put in a good word for you and try to explain what happened. I'll even add that you've been having a tough time at home."

"Thank you. I truly do appreciate the help. I'll be forever grateful to you if my job is somehow saved."

Hunger pangs begin. It's loud enough to be heard a mile away. The ice cream didn't seem to satisfy it last night. Mom bought me the cutest, most embarrassing bathing suit. I get super shy when going out with it on. Sometimes, it feels like the whole world is watching. I often forget what to do with my hands in awkward situations. My baby pink glistening onesie showed just enough skin to make my face turn bright red. What if someone from church sees me wearing it? Or worse, someone from work. Luckily, there's a skirt attached with shorts underneath, just in case the wind blows. My dark, curly hair seems to flow perfectly with it. It's my safety net when it comes to hiding my chest area. Being the conservative girl I am, long sleeves with sweatpants seem to be a more suitable option. But then I'd be even more out of place.

"Don't forget shampoo and conditioner," Sarah reminds me.

For some reason, my hair despises the salt water and sand. My scalp can get extremely itchy with the stinky smell of seaweed. Shea butter shampoo for wavy hair is the only one that can be used on it. Anything else creates white flakes, making it look as if I haven't washed my hair for weeks.

Sarah urges me to hurry so that we can find a good spot on the sand. The beach does get packed with people during this time of day. But the weary feeling from yesterday has not gone away, and I'd prefer to stay in my apartment and simply do nothing. That could potentially make me feel much better, but at the same time, spending the day all alone only brings on endless negative thoughts.

"Eve, come on, let's roll. Others are waiting for us." Sarah glares at me.

I gasp. "Huh? Who's waiting?"

"It's a surprise. You'll see."

We climb into Sarah's car at last after two hours of getting myself ready physically and emotionally. Surprises annoy me. When people think something is spectacular, it normally ends up being a disappointment for me.

The vehicle smells pleasant as we climb in, the crisp aroma of cherry and pineapples suggesting that she likely had this plan to make me come to the beach. Sarah owns a very old Jeep Wrangler, the kind that has to be taken to the shop every other day to get something fixed. However, it's got tons of charm. At certain times of the year, the outer shell is removed, exposing the entire Jeep to the outside world. It can be quite dangerous if you're not careful, but the wind flowing in the hot summer is worth it.

South Beach is already extremely crowded. It's one of those places that a lot of younger people go to, as well as families who have their children at home for summer vacation. There is one area where people go strictly at night where they can be in the nude as they please. We try to avoid that at all costs and end up leaving before the sun recedes into the water. I grab our towels and head towards the hot sand. The bottoms of my feet feel like the skin is boiling off. My friends, there they are, saving the best spot on the entire beach–right by the shore but far enough not to get drenched by the merciless salt water.

"Yo! Did you manage to lure Eve out of her cave?" asks Noah, his voice with an air of playful curiosity. He is the guy who captured Sarah's heart for the past few years. She keeps pushing her feelings aside, fearing that admitting the truth might make their friendship weird. I feel completely out of my depth. After all, I'm still waiting for my first kiss, and I'm hardly the one to offer any relationship advice.

Sarah wears a proud look on her face. "Yep! Leave it to me."

"Yeah, girl, you need to get out more. Your social skills are going to worsen if you keep letting work control your life!" Elizabeth exclaims, giving me a massive hug as if she hasn't seen me in a decade.

"Yeah, right. Easier said than done. Who else has something to say to me?" I grumble. People telling me what to do all the time gets old, but I low-key appreciate the advice.

"Guys, leave her be. Stop trying to control the situation. Let her feel if she wants to feel," James argues. I smile at him.

James is the only one in our friend group who is level-headed. The shy side dominates his personality, but he has significantly broken down those barriers since Sarah invited him to our group during our junior year of high school at lunchtime. Shyly and reluctantly, he introduced himself to all of us when Elizabeth started to challenge whether he was worth being friends with. She asked him all kinds of questions, like what his hobbies were, where he lived, what his parents did for a living, and what kind of food he enjoyed. It was quite an awkward experience to watch, but he passed the test. He belonged right away in our weird little group. Little did I know that the five of us would continue our friendship even into adulthood.

Meeting Elizabeth happened completely by accident and luck. In fact, she used to be the type of person who was unapproachable and obnoxious. In my sophomore year of high school, she sat next to me in Chemistry. I had no intention of ever speaking to her or introducing myself. After two weeks of silence, we had a group project. Everyone else already had friends in the classroom and a partner assigned. Since she and I didn't have one, we were forced to pair up.

"You know, don't assume that I'm ever going to talk to you again after this project," she clarified loud and clear. It was quite offensive.

"Fine with me." I kept our conversation as brief as possible.

The numbers danced in my mind as I jotted down answers with a sense of urgency. Two hours left until the project had to be at least somewhat complete, and it felt as if time was dragging on endlessly. My focus was unwavering until, finally, Elizabeth broke the silence.

"Wow, you're pretty smart. Where did you learn that?" She'd been watching me the entire time.

"Well, I've been paying attention in class and studying hard every single day. My dad's also very good with equations and used to challenge me growing up," I said spitefully, feeling proud of my family heritage for breaking through the stereotypes.

"Huh, is that so? Well, I like the sarcastic, proud attitude you have. Want to eat lunch together?"

"Sure."

After that, we naturally bonded. I realized that I had completely misjudged her. Eli had just moved in from New York City when her dad received a new, higher-paying job offer in Miami. Her mother didn't want to leave the state since they had family there, and the situation was going to turn their world upside down. Elizabeth was upset about her parents forcing her to move from the place she loved, feeling that no one was hearing her voice. Even her friends tried their best to be sympathetic, but she perceived their sympathy as an indication that they wanted her to leave. Sarah and I did everything we could to make Miami her new home. The three of us have had many good times together.

I glance around, scared of being observed in my embarrassing bathing suit. Families and sunbathers, engrossed in their own little worlds, take space in every nook and cranny of the beach. In my defense, no one stares at me, indicating it's safe to head to the water. Why am I so self-conscious all the time?

Sarah grunts. "Oh no... Maybe we should leave."

In shock, I respond, "How come?"

"Don't be scared, but look over there."

Lucas.

CHAPTER 3

I dive behind Sarah. Standing on the beach with that horrid smile is Lucas, the one I hate. Beaming at me with cold eyes, he comes up to our group, inviting himself to our get-together. The nerve of that guy. Isn't it enough to be bothered by him every day at work? The opportunity to run back to the car expires as he starts talking.

"Hey guys! Funny seeing you here," he yells loudly with his hands around his lips, creating an annoying horn effect.

No one dares to respond. He needs to know that he's not welcome in our bubble. Noah, the only one to break the ice, produces awkward small talk. The goal, I assume, is to make him take a hint and skedaddle away. But the plan fails miserably. Lucas brings over all of his belongings and places them right next to the space we've chosen on the sand. There's got to be something wrong with his head. *There's no way I can stay here with this creep.* He has so much pride with no regard for the feelings of anyone else. It's sickening.

"Whoa, guys, loosen up! Let's have some fun!" Lucas shouts as though he's completely unaware of the discomfort he's already brought to the group. His presence has always been unwelcome because of the way he treats others.

Gliding past the annoyance, I place my towel onto the wet sand, much closer to the water. My mind swirls, attempting to come up with ideas on how to run away. James stays by my side just in case Lucas comes over to bother me. Is there anything that could possibly make this day any worse?

"Eve, would you like me to put some sunscreen on your back? I wouldn't want you to get burned like last time," James kindly offers.

"Yes, please, that would be amazing." I accept the help gladly. Last time, my nose and shoulders burned so badly that the skin peeled off, healing in the weirdest way possible. My skin never looked the same after that. It left me with a weird blob shape, making it seem like I got a tattoo. Bumpiness can be felt when it's touched. Thank goodness it doesn't itch. My doctor said that it might go away in the future as long as that spot doesn't get any exposure to direct sunlight. But how? I live in Florida. That's nearly impossible.

The sunscreen provided a refreshing coolness that contrasted with the warm sunlight. James has the perfect amount of strength to be a professional masseuse. The man is also very good-looking. Back in high school, James wore big circular spectacles that made him look quite dorky. Elizabeth saw something in him, giving him advice to ditch the glasses for contact lenses. Then boom, a hidden gem appeared.

My back is sore from sitting in the chair at work for multiple hours without taking a break. Being a hard worker is my nature. Yet, sometimes, this dedication feels like a heavy weight on my well-being. Overthinking in the middle of the night about whether I completed certain work tasks plagues me. I slide my headphones in and let the music deepen the soothing feeling from the massage. Suddenly, Lucas storms over, clearly baffled by why James's gentle, soft hands are lingering on my shoulders. *Here we go again.* The moment of tranquility is instantly shattered. *Lord, give me patience.*

"Look, pal, I don't know who the heck you think you are, rubbing sunscreen on her. Did she even ask you to do that?" Lucas warrants defensively. Why would he care?

"Well, no, but I didn't want her to get sunburnt since it happened the last time we came here. I'm doing her a favor, of course," James says shyly, blushing.

Fury builds up in the face of Lucas as he turns completely red. He forcefully grabs James by the neck, squeezing tightly. I hear James struggling for air as he is launched into the sand.

I scream to the top of my lungs, "Stop, please. Don't hurt him!"

I run over to James to make sure he is okay. Fighting back isn't an option. Lucas is a strong and very violent person. There's no reasoning with someone who is never planning to change. Tears run down as I think about what could have happened. James could have been seriously hurt because of me.

"Same as usual, huh, Eve? You still don't have the guts to stand up to me."

"Please, leave us alone," I beg.

"All right, fine. I'll go. But don't think for a second about being even a minute late on Monday morning. I'm not doing any more favors for you."

Lucas grabs his stuff angrily and kicks sand at everyone as he walks away to a different part of the beach. What has gotten into that guy? His mood goes from happy to angry in an instant. There's no logic in any of it. I turn over with my back facing up to the sky and close my eyes to try to forget about Lucas.

Cool rain splashes against my cheeks. I twirl and dance to the rhythm of the rain, and sweet birds whistle from one side of the jungle to the other, where their mates wait expectantly. Surrounded by the lush greenery of the jungle, the vibrant colors of the flora add to the scene. I feel undeniably alive. A man with a shadowy face wraps his arms tightly around me. It feels right as if this is my destiny. Who is he?

"Eve. Eve. Wake up!" James shakes my arm until I return to the real world.

"What?! I was having an amazing dream." I pout.

"Well, there's something moving on your back."

A piercing yelp erupts from my throat, a raw expression of panic. "Get it off me!"

My hands swat at my back, trying to shoo away the squeamish creature. The feeling of disgust overshadows me as I feel the hand of James brush against my back, searching intently for any evidence of an insect.

"Eve, it's gone," he says.

"What happened?!" Sarah shrieks.

"There was something on my back!"

"Wow, girl, it's just a bug. It sounded like you were being abducted."

As the sun descends into the water, we all know that it's time to leave.

"Hey guys, we ought to leave before naked people start lurking here," Sarah warns.

Thankfully, Sarah is so mindful of the time. Being near the ocean brings a sense of forgetfulness to the real world. The bliss of being in the sun and listening to the ocean breeze makes me never want to leave. James and Elizabeth start to pack up the umbrella and the rest of the gear we brought.

Finally, home from the chaos, I hop into the shower, attempting to remove all the sand from my hair. That's one of the biggest problems with going to the beach. The fact that sand gets into every crevice and is extremely hard to remove. Even the bathtub gets drenched with the sand stuck to my toes. I know that the small beads will still be felt in my toes a week from now.

In my pajamas, I ponder the idea of traveling, conquering

my fears of insects. Something like that would only be possible in a dream. Mom's been dying to have a proper Sunday together with me for a while. I've been avoiding it for no reason except trying to hide from the fact that I need to make better decisions. She's been worried sick about me and has begged me multiple times to move back home. Quitting my job did sound like a good idea. I mean, there really isn't anything left for me. There's nothing to lose. Except I've got bills to pay. But I wouldn't at my parents'.

My alarm is set for 6:30 a.m. so that I won't miss church tomorrow. The past couple of Sundays have been tough. I didn't have the motivation to even want to get out of bed or talk to anyone. But one thing is certain: my faith has to stay strong. God has done so much for me up to this point in my life. Growing up in a Christian church that had tons of drama, my parents always told me to be careful about whom I share my personal life with. I couldn't understand why until I ended up getting in trouble with a couple of different preteens within the youth group. My insolence forced us to have to leave that church completely, even though my father had made many friends. I thought there was no hope for me to be in a place where I belonged.

In junior high, I cracked open a bible at the library and started reading it. Some of the stuff in there was very relatable, and the translation was much easier to understand than the old King James version they preached at that old church. Praying became a habit on a regular basis. It made things easier to cope with. Being the only child was also not exactly easy. My parents had such high expectations of me. Studying hard was a given, along with getting good grades and going straight to Harvard after graduation. In the real world, it doesn't work that way for everyone.

Leaving high school left me very uneasy, not being able to do what they wanted me to. I didn't have a clue what in the world to do with my life. I figured starting off working in an office setting would be a piece of cake, and then eventually working my way up the ranks. I've heard of many success stories where someone started from the bottom and eventually became the CEO of a company. It's motivating to see that there's hope for someone like me.

But then life throws you a Lucas, making running away easy. He has always had a bad attitude. Since we were in elementary school, he had some kind of bone to pick with me. All I know about him is that he was taken away from his parents at a young age. No one has guided him throughout his life, which is why he acts the way he does. I feel sorry for him most days of the week, but there is no amount of "sorry" that could get me to mend the damage he has done in my life. He used to chase me with bugs, squish their guts out into my hair, and start rumors about me.

Making friends was very difficult for the first half of my life. Everyone knew me as the loser who was terrified of everything. I begged my mom to take me out of that school so that I could be as far away from Lucas as possible, but we both knew that wouldn't be possible with our family income at the time. There isn't a real choice when it comes to public schools. It's based on the location and distance from the school. Transferring to a different school is only possible if the entire family moves to a different location. Homeschooling was also out of the question since they both had to work to afford the lifestyle they'd built.

My dad tried to cheer me up as much as possible. He started to notice that I was staying to myself more often and not engaging with other kids.

"Mija, go and make some friends. I wouldn't want you to be lonely." Dad would tell me this because it wasn't normal to be alone in Cuban culture. What he failed to understand was everything I went through in school. Teachers attempted to reprimand Lucas anytime they saw him bullying me or other people. When they tried calling his parents, no one had the answer to his terrible behavior. My dad eventually talked to my teacher about the problems at a parent-teacher conference.

"She has not stood up for herself yet and needs to gain the right amount of confidence to do so," my first-grade teacher told him.

"Is there anything we can do to help this situation? Can we put her in a different class, maybe?" Dad pleaded.

"Making a choice like that might only damage her further. Evelyn needs to see the problem in front of her and face it. Putting her into another class can promote procrastination and running from problems instead of solving them."

"Okay, I understand. What about contacting the boy's parents?"

"I've already tried reaching them and have not gotten any response quite yet. But I will continue disciplining as much as possible and keeping the two separated."

I remember every detail of this conversation because the adults were talking as if they knew what was best for me. All I wanted to do was run away. But instead, I was forced to endure all the bullying and hazing from Lucas and other kids in the class. It was quite lonely. Until the season of puberty came.

CHAPTER 4

*J*unior high was a game-changer. I had the fresh start that I had been wanting for years. Classes were separated into blocks, and many different students were around. I met Sarah in class a few weeks after school started in August. She and I were the only ones who did not know anyone, although I knew Lucas. I tried my best to stay out of his radar and to myself. Sarah asked me if I wanted to eat lunch together, which was shocking because no one had ever asked me that before. Normally, I would grab my lunch and find a corner away from all the obnoxious individuals. Seeing everyone else laughing and having great conversations made me feel like an empty husk that didn't deserve happiness.

During lunch, we both talked shyly about our interests. Trust was immediately developed as I told her all about my fears of bugs, talking to people, and being alone. I also told her about the things I enjoyed doing, like dancing, swimming at the beach, and listening to music. Turns out we shared the same interests. From one second to another, we became best friends.

Every day, I looked forward to spending time with Sarah. She was the only one to understand my dilemmas and worries about becoming a teenager. My mom told me ahead of time that one day, blood would start coming out of my bottom. I wasn't really sure what she meant by that. No one ever talked about those things, so I had no idea what was going on. When I turned thirteen, I peed in the toilet, wiped, and there it was—the magical dark red blood that Mom had mentioned a few months before. An unquenched amount of pain in my stomach came about even though I had eaten a huge dinner. I yelled for help, but it was too late; Mom was already asleep and had to be at work early the next day. I didn't want to be that person to make a bad day worse when her line of work already required a lot out of her. Instead, I leaned on Sarah. She immediately knew exactly what to do in the meantime.

"Go to the kitchen and grab some bananas, chocolate, and tissues," she told me on the phone.

"Okay, but what exactly are these going to do?" I said with dramatic pain in my voice.

"Just do it! You'll thank me later. I've got to go; my mom is yelling at me to go to bed. See you at school tomorrow."

I slowly rolled to the kitchen like a dying snail, holding my stomach as if that would make the pain better. It felt like there was an alien about to come bulging out. After grabbing all the requested items, I sat on my bed and understood immediately what these items were for. The banana was to help with cramps and solve my hunger pangs. The chocolate was going to make me feel happy because who doesn't like chocolate? The tissues were for wiping my tears from crying through the pain and putting some in my underwear until I could figure out what to do tomorrow. I couldn't go to school like that.

Eventually, I fell asleep.

Mom was extremely mad at me that morning for not waking her up. She explained what a period is, why it happens, and what needs to be done about it. She gave me a pack of pads and showed me exactly how to put them in my underwear. It felt like I had a bag in my pants, and I weighed five hundred pounds. The amount of acne I started to produce was unbearable. Luckily, Sarah knew exactly what to do for this too. Her mom was much better at explaining puberty before it happened instead of just giving a warning and waiting until I was in the thick of it. I swore that when I'm older and have children, I would tell them right away what's going to take place. Of course, Lucas, being in the same middle school, made his way to make fun of the zits on my face. Except this time, I had someone to be my backbone. Sarah did not tolerate his abusive words and did not allow him to stomp all over me, although he made fun of her, too.

Eventually, Noah came into the picture. A tall, dark, handsome guy that all the girls liked. He, too, was shy at first, which is why we were drawn to him. We didn't want anyone to feel out of place or lonely. These were the people we looked for. Noah was extremely grateful that we asked him to hang out with us; if not, he had planned to go to the basketball field and just chill there alone on the bleachers. Middle school is one of those places where you cannot be seen alone. People tend to look down on loners and not do anything to fix the problem. I immediately knew Noah was the perfect match for Sarah. He had this sweet, caring personality that reminded me of my father. His biggest skill is understanding non-verbal cues. He can tell when someone is sad, happy, annoyed, or simply needs time to themselves. I've made a few acquaintances along the way, just girls trying to get close to Noah until they realize that he isn't interested in anyone at all. Or so he would tell people. But I've seen the way he looks at Sarah, with those passionate, loving eyes.

As I reminisce on all these memories, I feel extremely grateful to have my friends and family in my life. None of us are anywhere near perfect, but life is much easier having like-minded people around. *Being friends for life is a huge goal.*

CHAPTER 5

J wake up to the most bizarre sounds.

Bang, boom, bop. The sound of power tools infest the air. What is going on? A knock on my door jolts me from bed. Hopefully, the apartment manager is here to give me some answers.

I get to the door and see that it is him. The apartment manager has wanted to chat with me for a while now to tell me that there were going to be renovations first thing on Sunday morning. All the other tenants were informed except for me, since I've dodged any meetings with any of the managers around. The neighbors could have told me, but I've been letting out tons of negative energy. They see me at least twice a day, once in the morning, then again when I come home for the day. There is no use worrying about why no one told me or why there were no signs of any construction work being done today. The noise is so unbearable that it forces me to get ready for church early without consuming any nutrients.

I step outside to my car and slide into the driver's seat in utter silence. That way, a migraine can't sneak up on me during the service. You can only take so much headache medicine before overdosing. Relying on medication each time there is pain ruins the immune system; at least, that's what my mom keeps reminding me. She's extremely old school when it comes to health issues. When something goes wrong, I get advice to drink a certain tea or to simply lie down in bed for a nice rest. Most of the tips that she gives me about any topic are pretty accurate; she has rarely ever been wrong.

I once brought a classmate home who I thought was going to be a potential good friend. My mom knew right away that something was odd about the girl and that one day, she would bring me great grief. In my mind, there was no freaking way she could know that by just talking to someone. I decided that I would wait for the moment to happen before judging a book by its cover. Turns out that my mom was completely right with the prediction. Gina went behind my back and told most of my secrets to other girls who hated my guts. When I stopped hanging out with her as much as I did, my mom started to realize that what she had predicted was indeed correct.

"Well, yo te dije, Mija," my mom bragged about being right with a smile on her face. It was the equivalent of, "I told you so!"

Arriving at church always feels good. The people who attend have always been extremely supportive. I'm very blessed to have found a good environment. We once went to a church that was awful. The many rules included not wearing a T-shirt or jeans. Women were not allowed to speak on stage or even participate in the daily prayer with everyone. I knew immediately that, as a family, a decision needed to be made about finding a new church home. I complained to my papa a few times, but he was blinded by the camaraderie he was able to attain. Eventually, he started to listen, and it was clear that we needed to leave. Miami has tons of multicultural churches now, but back then, there were none. Diversity in a church was completely unheard of. White folks would go to Methodist churches. Black folks would go to Baptist churches. Asians would form their own churches.

Lastly, Latinos ended up being shunned from Greek Orthodox churches and encouraged to create their own Spanish-speaking congregations. It made it very hard to find a good place to be, one that enforced unity as one body of Christ.

The current church that we attend came into our lives after searching for months. A small church in the middle of nowhere with people who have to drive more than an hour to get there. But the drive is worth it. The amount of love we all have received here is unfathomable. There are multiple translators on duty to satisfy multicultural needs. The main pastor speaks and preaches in English; however, the church offers a pre-recorded podcast in different languages for people to listen to while in service. This allows for the full experience of going to church and being able to understand. There are also multiple screens in the very front of the platform that display the translation with words as he is speaking. The translators are there to pray for people and answer any questions they may have. All races are welcome and accepted. Even gays and lesbians are not shunned but invited in. It's exactly what I picture when Jesus says to love all people and to serve them.

I get to my parents' house kind of late because of traffic, which is the usual amount in South Florida in the morning. There's not one time that I plan something and am actually early. It's become such a custom that everyone in my life expects me to be at least an hour late. I always leave home slightly early, but it must be the way I drive. Since my grandma was the one who taught me how, I guess I've taken on her ethics of the road. I tend to stay on the right, slow lane, except while passing. Driving has always been nerve-wracking. I make sure there are at least two car spaces in front of me and behind me, just in case someone decides they need to check their phone or put makeup on in the middle of the highway. Seriously, these things really do happen daily. It's kind of sad.

"Where have you been? We're super late. This is so embarrassing," my mom says as soon as she opens the front door to let me in. She rushes us all out of the house so that we can be on our way.

The view of the parking lot of our church building finally allows us to breathe when we arrive an hour later, knowing that we were not the only ones who were late. No one has ever said anything about it being a problem. It's just a fact that we must all accept that living here means being late all the time. It comes with residing in a large city with overcrowded roads. One of the pastors welcomes us at the door, as always, and invites us to drink some free coffee in the lobby. *Don't mind if I do.* It's the best treat I've had all week long. The mugs hang on the wall. They are free to borrow during the service but must be washed and put back when finished.

After church, I'm very curious about the funds my mom spoke of on the phone. It isn't surprising that they would keep something like this from me. Throughout my life, they have surprised me on many different occasions. Once, a few days before my birthday, a puppy was hidden from me for an entire week. I wondered why my dad kept making his way outside for long periods of time. All I wanted to do was go outside to play, but I had to wait until he returned. None of it made any sense. During the night, I even started to hear whimpering in our yard, which sounded like a ghost. My parents seemed off, but I couldn't figure out what was going on. Finally, my birthday arrived, and the little puppy showed up. To my knowledge, I did not necessarily ask for a dog; it was what my dad wanted. Nonetheless, I was ecstatic.

We make a stop at a Cuban Café that we eat at quite often. All of the classics that I adore are on the menu, including croquettes, pastries, ham sandwiches, and, of course, delicious café con leche, which I probably won't order since I had my fair share of coffee at church. Too much caffeine gives me the jitters.

I order my favorite, a batch of croquettes, as we pick a cozy spot to go over my mom's proposal.

"So, let's talk. You have a fund for me that I didn't know anything about?" I question with a huge smile on my face.

"Si Mija, por unos años," my mom explains that it's been a few years now.

"Huh. So why didn't anyone tell me about this?"

"We weren't sure if you were ready for the money quite yet. We, of course, wanted you to attend Harvard, but after you told us that you don't want to study, we put the money on hold in the account. That way, it can continue producing revenue," my dad chimes in on the situation at last. I could not believe that my parents thought so far as to save money for my college life.

It's by far the sweetest thing that anyone has ever done for me. As soon as I left for the first time at eighteen years old, I knew how hard it was going to be to get by, with the cost of living skyrocketing randomly based on the economy and the market. Finding out the monthly cost of an apartment and a new vehicle was not easy. Bills started piling up to the point that college had been categorized as too expensive. Most organizations wanted a full-time employee. Part-timers get robbed of hours. There was no way I could balance a full-time job and going to school at the same time. Plus, a nice break was necessary from the get-go. After being treated the way I had for many years, I thought taking a break would be just what was needed to fuel a spark in my life.

"Ma, I honestly still don't see any reason to go to college. But please, please, please, allow me to travel for a while. I need to see the world. I feel stagnant here," I beg. Being understood is my goal here. Although it rarely happens. *Please be understanding.*

They both stay silent for a while, get up, and go outside to talk. My hands begin to jitter at the possibility of the idea getting rejected. After about twenty minutes, my beloved parents return, taking a seat. They look up at me with huge smiles, making my heart flare with animation. What are they about to tell me?

"After some talking, your papa and I have decided that we would be willing to fund your adventure as long as you promise us that as soon as you get back, you will stop this madness and create a solid plan for your life."

"Oh, my goodness. Yes. Deal."

The preparations begin. My parents tell me that they need to be kept in the loop at all times. That's a lot of expectations to uphold.

The pressure to tell Sarah the plan makes me nervous. She's my best friend, so I have to. We tell each other everything. I wouldn't want her hiding anything from me.

"You're doing what?!" she argues.

"I need to conquer my fears. Staying here is only stopping me from being the person God has called me to be," I explain.

"What if something happens? I'm scared of losing you."

"You won't lose me. I have Christ on my side. What could go wrong?"

The bosses sit at the large table in the back. It feels like being interrogated by a lawyer. They ask me to take a seat to chat for a few minutes. Initially, I planned on putting in my two weeks with respect to all that they have done for me. But then thoughts started to flood my mind of being harassed by Lucas. I didn't want to put myself in that situation willingly.

"So, rumor has it that you are going on a trip?" Mr. Ledger asks me bluntly. I guess nothing in this place stays hidden. I only told one person, so I guess that's who the culprit is.

"Yes, sir, I'm embarking on a journey. Looks like I don't have enough vacation time. Therefore, I will also be leaving the company," I explain as kindly and politely as possible.

"I see. What a shame to lose such a great worker. If you ever do decide to come back, here is my card. We'd be pleased to have someone with such talent back on the team."

"You got it. Thank you so much for understanding." I walk out of the office as quickly as possible to avoid my coworkers, but it's too late. They are already trying to convince me to stay. Even Sarah couldn't convince me when we spoke yesterday. Lucas catches me on the way out of the office door and pulls me to the side.

"Hey, uh, there's something I need to tell you," Lucas says all shyly as if something has been bothering him.

"Uh-huh?" I respond nonchalantly. It's not like there is anything this guy could say that would stop me from walking out that door. With bags in my hand and my company shirt turned in, it finally feels like it's truly happening.

"Listen, I'm sorry for the way I've treated you. But I have to admit something I've been holding in all my life." He takes a deep breath. "Eve, I really love you."

In shock, extremely confused about what to say, my hand flings over my lips. What just came out of his mouth? My brain is completely foggy at the moment. There is no way that he and I could ever work as a romantic couple. I hate him. He hates me. All of the actions up to this point have led me to believe that. Why now? Why this?

"Are you out of your mind? Maybe you need to sit down," I work up the courage to say.

"No, it's the truth. I followed you to this job because one day, I wanted to get my life together to become a good man for you."

"You've got to be kidding me. I need to go." I storm out the door and run towards my car, not believing what just happened. There's no way this is real!

CHAPTER 6

$\mathcal{T}$he nerve of that guy! After all that he's done to me, there's no way that I could ever accept his feelings. There has never been any indication of any kind of love running through his bones. The amount of people that have been crushed by his ego can't even be counted with both hands. He's the main reason why I have to leave. I can't stand the thought of continuing to work at that job being threatened each day, causing my confidence to lower more and more. Lucas has been kissing the butt of the bosses since he began working here and even stole the managerial opportunity that I had been praying for. It was the position that would have made me feel important and valued within the company. Mr. Ledger has been kind to me for the last few years yet has not given me a reason to stay. If he truly cared, he would have tried to convince me not to go. I know what needs to be done, and my parents have provided a way out of this. Lucas can't stop me.

Arriving home, I feel extremely overwhelmed with tears in my eyes. How could someone so abusive have the audacity to choose to continue this cycle even after realizing their feelings? It's sick. Now, I know that Lucas has had issues with family in the past. My parents and different rumors at school confirmed his unfortunate upbringing. That still isn't any excuse. I don't even know how to feel right now. The horrid feelings of disgust, hatred, and compassion all come out at once. I'm left extremely confused. I decide to skip dinner since eating would only make me throw up. My appetite is based on what's going on at the current moment. When I'm super happy, hunger is intense. When I'm sad or fearful, meals are skipped for multiple days. Other emotions are dependent on how fast the situation is fixed and how minimal or significant it is.

After an hour of settling down on the couch, I hear knocking on my door. Oh no, why would anyone come to bother me now? The day is hard enough to get through. I get up lazily with no more energy to deal with anything else today. Luckily, it's Sarah.

"Hey, girl. I heard what happened. You okay?" she asks with the softest, most compassionate voice. That job isn't going to get me anywhere in life. I felt stuck the entire time.

"Yeah, I'm doing all right. It was time for me to go," I respond confidently. I'm not going to lie; not having an income can be frightening. But who cares? Soon, I'll be on my way to the first spot on my bucket list.

"That's not what I mean. I'm talking about Lucas."

I bet Lucas went around telling everyone in the office what happened. He doesn't seem to have a filter.

"Oh, that. He told you?"

"Honey, I've known for many years now that he has had the biggest crush on you."

"But how did you know? Why did you not tell me?"

"Because I knew that you hated him. It would only have made things weird. Sometimes 'boys' mistreat the girls they like but later on come out with their feelings."

"Yeah, it doesn't work that way. He has never once been

pleasant to be around. There is no way I'd ever give him a chance," I hiss angrily.

"Okay, that's understandable. But at least as a human being, can you try to forgive him? Resentment is not good for the soul."

Forgive him? After all that he has done? *No freaking way!* I have so many bad memories in the arsenal that I still haven't even told her or my own parents about. Lucas used to slam me into the hallway walls, start random rumors about me sleeping around so that I could never catch a date with anyone, and even put bugs in my bag and clothes. Putting a restraining order on him sounds wonderful, not dating him! But as a Christian, I wouldn't want to make his situation worse. I know very well about his mother and the abuse he underwent from different foster families, including sexual abuse.

"Sarah, let me think about that for a while, okay? This is all a ton to take in. I'll keep in touch, but I really have to get to bed, please?"

"Okay, no problem. I just wanted to make sure that you aren't going through all of this alone. I'm here for you. Let's go out somewhere soon."

Sarah is one of a kind. I appreciate it so much when she comes over to check on me. She always provides the advice that I require at the perfect time. Sarah isn't the type to simply agree with what everyone says just to make someone feel better. Her thoughts and opinions are genuine.

My head is best cleared after the worries of the day get washed down the drain. A hot shower should do the trick. I lie my head on my fluffy pillow, feeling extremely excited about my upcoming trip. Normally, I'd be freaking out about planning, but after being super nervous about quitting my job and Lucas telling me his feelings, I'm drained.

My feet move on their own. I'm terrified. Thousands of beetles come at me, running to devour my flesh. I run as fast as I possibly can, making a sharp left turn at the corner with a view of the exit up ahead. Adrenaline takes over my body when suddenly there's a clear film blocking the way out. I pound on that thing, using my nails to rip through it. There's no use.

My eyes pop open. *Gross!* I awaken terrified, yet extremely grateful that it's not actually real. These fears are going to somehow hinder my journey. If I see a giant bug, what if I run away and waste the entire opportunity? I can't back down now. If I work up the courage and have faith, everything is going to be just fine.

I write down a few destinations I want to go to. Choosing is so difficult. It makes me super nervous. Scheduling multiple tour guides is a must. That way, I'm not alone the whole time. If only someone could come with me, but that's way too much to ask for. Trips are expensive, and not everyone can take time off work to do this. I'm very blessed and lucky to have the opportunity. If Sarah could come with me, it wouldn't feel so lonely. Although she'd have to fund her own trip and miss three weeks of work. It might be a problem if she can't pay her bills. I decide to send a text anyway. It's not going to hurt anyone if she says no. It's better to ask and know than not to ask and wonder what if.

Me: Hey Sarah, I have a huge favor to ask of you.

I wait with great anticipation for her reply, even though I know she's at work, struggling to stay awake and dealing with Lucas and his impossible demands. Other office administrators have been pulling the work for my old financial advisor since I left the company. I miss my team, but at the same time, this is good for them.

Sarah: Hey Eve, what's up?

Me: Can you please come with me on this trip?

Sarah: Uh, with what money?

Me: Come on, you have to have some money saved up after all this time!

Sarah: No, I really don't. I'm sorry, Eve. Good luck!

Should I be mad? Absolutely not. This journey is mine alone. It's to be expected. If I'd asked anyone else, they'd probably also say no. Sarah is the only person that I would want to travel with. We have very similar interests, making going places easier. When there is a will, there is always a way. I only have enough money to fund my tickets, lodging, food, and excursions with the travel guides. I'll have to make an effort to keep a close eye on my expenditures.

CHAPTER 7

*T*he airport in Sydney is a little confusing compared to the ones back home, but at least there are signs everywhere and a guard watching over the people to make sure no one does anything funky. I peek out the giant window on the way to the baggage area. Wow. The view is gorgeous. The way that the sunbeams shine over the ocean is very close to where all the planes are taking off. I request an Uber ride to the hotel after spending almost an hour trying to locate my bags. I'm super grateful that the person driving did not bother to make conversation. The capacity to think about what I need to talk about is out of the question.

My mind wanders with the amazing sights to see. Not to mention, the weather is slightly cooler during this time of the year. I wonder if my hair will poof up or not since the air is as dry as can be. There were a couple of people in my high school who moved to Florida from the Midwest. The humidity alone messes with the way people breathe. My skin loves it. It can be difficult to adapt from one environment to another without exposure and practice. The tall skyscrapers remind me of

Miami, but at the same time, have the charm of New York that I've only seen in movies.

I come to the realization that I am completely alone. I hope that Sarah is going to be okay without me for a few weeks. She's been dealing with a lot of complications with her family since she became an adult. Her parents split up after she moved out. The news came out of nowhere one day. Her parents explained that they hadn't been happy the entire time they were married. Those two would be phenomenal actors since they did such a great job hiding their problems so that they could be a good example to their children. There was no indication that something was ever wrong.

Sarah's dad had been having an affair with his coworker all that time and is currently living happily with his other family now that her siblings are all grown up and out of the house. As for Sarah's mom, she fled Florida immediately to pursue her lifelong dream of becoming a clothing designer. It's so sad that they were unhappy for so many years and thought they had to stay together even when they didn't want to. All the times I went to visit Sarah during our years together in high school, her mom was such a kind person, always giving us advice about relationships and finding happiness in Christ alone. She seemed to be a person that I could always come to when I needed help in my own life.

When things went south after the divorce, Sarah needed all the love and help that she could get. I was there through the days when her family resented their father for what he did. He showed no remorse or regret about it. Where we live in Miami, there are many temptations that need to be resisted. Too many bars, drugs, and access to clubs. A strong will is needed to survive in a city of the lost, similar to Las Vegas, or so I've heard. Sarah's mom has not reached out to any of her children. She wanted a break from all those years of misery. I've made multiple attempts to email, call, and even send mail, but so far, I haven't gotten any response. I know that Sarah is extremely worried about her parents. She needs them even if she is an adult.

The hotel is a big, tall building that looks like it has over twenty-four floors. The front desk employee greets us with a huge smile. Her super cute accent catches my attention.

"Welcome in, mate!"

To check in, all I had to do was show the QR code that was provided this morning through email confirmation.

The bellhop asks if I need any help bringing my bags upstairs to which I decline the offer. Instead, he hands me a door key, pointing in the direction of the elevator leading to my home for the week. The smells of citrus puff in the air. I can tell lemon products were used to keep the place clean. I love that smell; it reminds me of my parents' house.

Oh, my goodness. This is seriously gorgeous!

I cannot believe my own eyes. I'm placed on the sixteenth floor. It makes me skeptical of being so high up, but the view is uncanny. The entire city can be seen from up here, along with the beautiful ocean. Even the bed is fluffy; the sheets are white as snow, looking like giant marshmallows have taken over the bed. *I can't wait to sleep!*

Two seconds after closing my eyes, the room phone rings with the most annoying sound ever. It would be a perfect alarm clock for someone who is a deep sleeper. Unfortunately for me, that's not the case. Light sleeping forces me to wake up, and any little sound, even a fly buzzing, can prevent me from sleeping the rest of the night after being disturbed. I hoist the phone to my ear.

"Yes, hello?" I let out, unintentionally grumpy.

"Sorry, ma'am, to intrude; the meal you ordered won't be ready for another hour. Is this okay?" a woman says with a super kind tone. There's no way I could stay angry at that.

"Actually, ma'am, I didn't order any room service."

"Oh, my apologies I must have gotten confused with the room next door."

Going back to sleep after that is definitely impossible. I wish I'd sounded a little kinder over the phone. It would have been much worse to have some stranger knocking on my door when I was trying to sleep.

According to Google, one of the most popular restaurants to be able to see the Sydney Opera House is a Korean restaurant close to the coast. I don't bother changing clothes. I get to the restaurant in sweatpants and a T-shirt. People look at me as if it's clear that I'm not from around here, as there are many tourists coming here year-round. In my book, the best time to go anywhere is when the right amount of funds is sitting pretty in my bank account. To get what I came here for, it needs to be hot enough for the bugs to be comfortable and cool enough for me to be able to go outside. As I sit down facing the large window showing the entire bay, I browse through the menu, not able to find any prices. I guess that means this meal is going to be expensive. I order the four-course meal so that I can get to try most of the things on the menu.

I devour the garlic bread, which calls my name as soon as the waiter puts it down on the table. It tastes delicious and is most likely going to make my breath rancid. My biggest pet peeve is being smelly. I'm in Australia now, so preventing stinginess is a must.

The waiter softly places the bill directly in the middle of the table, as if he were worried that I wouldn't be able to pay. I pick it up, almost choking on my drink. A whopping 190 Australian dollars. The waiter knows something is wrong from the dreadful look on my face. He comes over to clear the negative air and answer my question. There's no way it could be this much. The waiter tells me that the calculation is correct, showing proof of the pricing on a secret menu that should have been here on the table the entire time. I feel so foolish for not asking about the price before making the order. At a loss, I hand the man my credit card, not wanting to cause a scene today. After all, there's no denying that the food was scrumptious. Made to perfection. I peek over at the Opera House, admiring the ocean view the most. It all feels like a dream.

I planned on saving a ton of money during this trip. That way, I could make it to the other two countries without needing to ask my parents for more money. I need to be more cautious with the restaurants I attend and things that are purchased on a whim. Instead of overthinking, I decide to forgive myself for the one-off mistake. A nap sounds wonderful right now since the lady up front woke me up earlier. I lie my head on the soft pillow and fall into a trance.

I'm holding on to the man I despise, Lucas. A few seconds ago, he got down to his knees, begging me for forgiveness, allowing tears to shed. The apology seemed genuine. He caresses my shoulder as he looks me in the eyes. No words come out. Lucas puckers his lips, aiming slowly toward mine. *No. No. This is wrong. It's not that easy.* My body freezes, not allowing me to run away from it. It is happening.

My eyes widen as I realize that it was only a dream. *Thank goodness.* My body is drenched in sweat, with my heart beating faster than ever. I'm millions of miles away from that creep. There's no way he'd be able to follow me here. Or would he?

CHAPTER 8

The Royal Botanical Garden is only about a five-minute walk from the hotel. Wow, it's amazing to see such beauty. Pictures don't do it any justice. Located right next to the Sydney Opera House, where the ocean's constant push and pull of the waves lap the shore. A few boats are in the water, either fishing or taking tourists on rides. People here seem to have it going right for them. Everyone looks so happy. They're in their own worlds, yet very connected with others.

I go in through the dazzling calyx entrance. Long vining plants with little yellow flowers hang from the ceiling, something that could only be imagined in a scary, man-eating-plant movie. Multiple houseplants take over the entire display. I'm the type who buys a plant, completely forgets about it, and comes back in two months in tears because I allowed it to die of thirst. After that spout, another plant ends up in my possession, but then that one dies from being overwatered. A snake plant might be the perfect addition to my apartment. It barely requires water, likes mostly sunlight, and grows regardless of its soil. Another name for it is "Mother-in-law's tongue." Hmm, I'd rather not know why it's called that.

The coral reef section is magical. It's like I am underwater without swimming. Diagrams containing different sea creatures that can survive with certain underwater plants remind me of aliens from movies, especially certain breeds of crabs. The thought that there are some who look more like bugs... *Yuck.* Sea worms, snails, and isopods aren't from this world. I shiver with goosebumps as I go through more exhibits.

Further into the garden, a stunning row of rose bushes takes hold of my attention. The fragrance hits the air, leading me to the best-smelling bush. It's a gardenia. White, soft petals with yellow spores in the center. *Mom would love this.* Yellow, red, and pink roses sparkle from the morning dew. Statues of art pose for pictures in different parts of the garden. Someday, when I'm much older, I'd like to start my own garden, with the proper training, of course. I would like to get to know the different plant life along with the bugs that nurture them. Bees terrify me. The way their wings buzz as they fly right past your face in a hurry to accomplish their mission of getting the pollen back to their hives. I remember from what my fourth-grade teacher taught me that they are extremely important for the planet. Plants can only reproduce because of the amazing, free job that bees do. But still...

James once got stung by one while we were having lunch in the middle of the day. We normally sat inside for lunch but decided it was too cold and crowded in the cafeteria. As we began to eat, one zoomed past us, then stopped and stung him right in the kisser. His face swelled up like a balloon while I ran to find the school nurse, who was delayed since she was dealing with an injured student. James' mom was not happy when she heard what happened, but luckily, it was nothing fatal. He was blessed to stay home for the remainder of the week with a doctor's note. No allergy was found, but the sting happened to be in a weird spot that took a while to heal. My fear only grew worse for bees after that.

On the way out of the botanical garden, I grab a blanket from my backpack and place it on the ground under a large tree, providing an abundance of shade. *I knew it would come in handy.* The view is amazing. The water glistens with the reflection of sunlight. Randomly, a guy walks up, taking a stance on the opposite side of the tree. Minding his own business, he beams at something resting on a twig. He seems like an introverted fellow who does not want to be bothered. In Florida, I got stared at often. Here, I barely got any looks. It's a nice change of pace.

I stand up, intrigued by the sound of camera shots, to see what this guy is up to behind the tree. I walk over, feeling an inexplicable pull to the mysterious man. He's nestled in the shadows, devoted to the clicks of the shutter button with precision. From a small distance, his notes go on and on endlessly. I bet he's a college student.

"Hello," I say shyly.

"Hi," he responds very awkwardly, holding his camera as if it were the love of his life.

"I noticed that you were taking pictures of something in the tree. Is there a bird?"

His eyes light up as he realizes that I'm interested in what he's working on so diligently.

"Actually, I'm taking close ups of this lychee stink bug. He is phenomenal."

"Oh, cool. May I take a look?"

"You might scare him if you get too close, but I can show you the photos I took."

He shows me this nasty, yellowish-green creature that almost looks like a giant tick. *Gross.* Looking at the hair on the legs gives me shivers. Zooming into the photo makes the effect ten times worse. Why? Why did I say yes without thinking?

"They come in many different colors depending on their stage in development," he says with a smirk.

"What has you so interested in this, er, thing?"

"I'm writing a paper in college about them and why they are so prominent to Sydney."

That's it. Bingo. What if this guy can show me more bugs? He can potentially teach me things that only a person fascinated by bugs would know about. It would make my fear subside a lot quicker than if I did all of this using my own methods. Looking intently, I notice that he's actually a very handsome man. Wow. Nerdy, yet totally my type. I blush.

"Hey, random question, I'm only here for a couple of days. Would you mind showing me more about these, er, magnificent creatures?"

He seems to debate this for a moment, likely deciding if I'm a creepy or normal kind of stranger. His smile returns and my heart beats faster in anticipation. "Sure! That would be great. Let's meet tomorrow afternoon, around 1:00 p.m., at the Australian Museum. They have a wonderful selection of insects we can study together," he says.

"Sounds great. And your name is?"

"Oh, I got so excited to tell you what I was doing that introducing myself slipped my mind. My name is Oliver, but you can call me Oli."

"Oli, huh? Great, I love nicknames. My name is Evelyn, but you can call me Eve. It's very nice to meet you." I reach over for a handshake, but instead, I get pulled in for a hug. My face burns cherry red.

Oli lets go of his grip with a chuckle. "Sorry about that. It's so exciting to meet someone else who has an interest in insects. I'll see you tomorrow at 1:00 p.m."

"See you then!"

Still blushing, I walk back to the hotel, jubilant. My hands jitter with nervousness. I've never successfully "flirted" with anyone in my life. And we flirted in the nerdiest way possible. *I can't believe I just did that!* Proud of myself, I fold up the blanket looking at the ground to try to calm myself down.

To me, this is a huge moment. A massive step forward in my journey of conquering my fear of bugs. It's also a confidence booster since Lucas always told me that no guy would ever consider going on a date with me. Hah. Who's laughing now?

CHAPTER 9

There's nothing like delicious biscuits with jam and coffee first thing in the morning. This is the life, for sure. No responsibilities, no bills, simply freedom. I know it's not forever, that sometime soon, I'll run out of money and have to go back home to the real world. But right now, who cares?

I grab my bag from upstairs and head outside towards the front of the hotel. Nervously, I call for a taxi since I'm already late meeting Oli at the bug museum. Of course. Leave it to the girl from Miami to be fashionably late. How could I do this on the most important date I've ever had? *Wait, a date?!* I turn red. I cannot believe this is happening for real.

The taxi shows up in no time, as I anticipated. The driver gets out of the front seat to open the door for me and asks for my destination.

When I get to the museum, Oli is standing outside, awaiting my arrival. From a distance, it looks like he fixed up his hair. It's not as shaggy and cute as it was yesterday. I feel tickled with nervousness as he waves hello. He has this nerdy charm and is bustling with confidence. *This is really happening.*

"Shall we?" he says calmly.

"Oh, yes. I'm very excited to learn," I respond, more inter-ested in getting to know him. We head to the entrance to learn that there is no fee for coming to visit. I'm shocked. That's unheard of in Miami.

"There are over 500,000 species in this collection. Isn't it exquisite?"

"Oh yes, of course it is. They are... er... beautiful," I lie.

One by one, we look into every case containing different kinds of colored beetles. Green, blue, red, orange, and yellow creatures that died for scientific purposes. Entomology is the study of insects. It's what Oli is studying in college, I learn. Now, the fly section. These disgusting little things. I've heard that when they land on your food, they lay their eggs and when you eat it, it grows in your stomach. I've also heard that they poop along with laying their eggs. Then again, it could just be an old grandma's tale to get young children to eat their food faster and finish it all so that there are no leftovers to throw away.

"Eve, take a closer look at their little heads; they all look completely different."

I peek inside the microscope and instantly feel chills. Flies have nasty-looking faces with giant eyes, almost like an alien from planet Mars. Oli is utterly fascinated by them while I'm absolutely nauseated. Seeing the enjoyment on his face makes me pumped up to continue conquering my fears, though.

The next section has a little praying mantis who is actually alive in his enclosure, not like the others. She's honestly adorable. Small and fierce, just like me. According to the description near the enclosure, thirty percent of the time, the female bites the head off the male while mating if she's hungry enough. They can also turn their heads 180 degrees. *That's quite dark.*

"Hey, Eve, check this out. Do you know how to determine

whether an animal is an insect?" Oli asks. Disgust has already petrified me, but having him talk to me makes it all better.

"I don't, but I would love to know," I respond.

"Insects are specific animals that have a pair of antennae, six walking legs, and a skeleton outside the body."

Instantly, I think of Lucas. I can't really consider him a bug since he doesn't have six legs, but it sure does seem as if he has a hard, bony skeleton on the outside and inside. I have never seen that guy show any positive feelings. Well, except for when he confessed his unbelievably masochistic love for me out of nowhere.

"Oh, cool. Thanks for sharing that."

At last, we reach the end of the museum, where the butterflies and moths belong. The owners planned the entire path, going from the most disgusting creatures to the prettiest ones. It all depends on the eyes of the beholder. Oli seems to have really enjoyed the ugliest, creepy crawlers. The butterflies are gorgeous in a wide range of shapes, sizes, and colors. My entire life, I thought that moths looked basic; that is until today. I realize that the butterflies I admire are actually moths. The difference between a butterfly and a moth is the antennae, the colors, the wings, their activity, and their resting postures. Moths are strictly nocturnal. Butterflies are more active during the day. Moths have dull colors, while butterflies have brighter colors. The average lifespan of a butterfly is two to four weeks, which is extremely sad to think of. Meanwhile, its moth cousin lives anywhere from forty-two to fifty-six days.

Why does time seem to fly when I'm having a great time? I thank Oli for the invite. Before I start finger-bumping my phone to call for a cab, Oli invites me to a nearby café that's very popular and filled with locals and college students. How could I refuse? Maybe he really is into me. *Now is the time.* The short walk to the café offers us a moment to get to know each other.

"So, uh, where are you from?" I shyly ask.

"Sydney, of course. Born and raised here," he says, allowing his accent to flow more than before. The words that come out of his mouth sound adorable.

"Ah, gotcha." I run out of things to say in a jiffy. Conquering my fear of asking someone on a date made me overconfident. It isn't common for a girl to ask a guy out. Actually, the act is frowned upon, although it shouldn't be. It's not any gender's responsibility to do one thing over the other. I notice that Oli can be just as weird as me. He doesn't mind having some silence. I can't wait to get to that level of not caring about being awkward.

The café looks very old yet remodeled from the inside to the outside. It's a small sandstone building that has been open since 1888. The aroma of delicious vanilla coffee excites my nose. It brings me back to a time when my dad and I used to wake up early on Saturday mornings to have breakfast together. Mom used this time to rest and recharge after a long week. My dad always had to have his *café con leche* with the delicious butter bread that could be dipped into the milky coffee for an even more pleasant experience. Bullies, including Lucas, made fun of me for dipping my bread into hot chocolate during breakfast in the cafeteria at school. Even my teachers would shun my behavior, but the reality was that doing so helped me cope with being away from home for so many hours. It's a friendly reminder not to shun the culture of others. Instead, make an effort to try to understand it by asking questions.

Oli orders the orange and honey waffle, which tells me that he has a sweet tooth. He'd fit into Cuban culture perfectly. I adore sweet things, but an avocado dish spoke to me. It kind of reminds me of home. My mom has an avocado tree in the backyard that she treats like my sibling. She planted it the day I was born and has nourished it ever since. Year after year, it continues to provide many delicious and prosperous avocados.

We take a seat by the window, overlooking the ocean with a perfect view of the golden late afternoon sun. What a beautiful and peaceful place this is. The thought of leaving scares me. Especially after meeting such a great guy. I feel completely at ease in his presence. Sarah would be so proud of me for stepping out of my comfort zone. This is just the beginning.

"Hey, thank you for inviting me today. I really enjoyed meeting you and showing you what I'm so passionate about. Let's do this again," Oli says with a full mouth of food.

"You really mean it?" I say with too much excitement as if I've accomplished a great victory.

"Yeah, next time, I'll bring my girlfriend Amelia. She'll be thrilled to meet someone who's as excited about insects as we are."

Wait. Did he just say girlfriend? *Oh, snap.* Of course, he's taken. There's no way such a charming and funny guy would be single.

"Yeah... right. Hey, I'll be right back. I need to use the restroom."

I get up because my heart feels like it got punched. This entire time, I thought that we were on a date! I assumed he was into me because of how sweet he was and the fact that I got invited to hang out some more after the museum.

Ashamed, I lock myself up inside the toilet stall. How can I face him after this? Fifteen minutes into pouting in the restroom, one of the waitresses comes to check up on me. How embarrassing.

"Hey, pretty lady, you alright?" she asks, concerned.

"Yes, ma'am," I say, lying through my teeth.

"I'm here if you need to talk. Your friend out there is quite worried about you. Come out when you can."

Deep breaths, Eve, deep breaths. All the makeup I put on this morning smudges down my cheeks as I wash my face with freezing cold water. It's not like me to put all that stuff on my face. I only did it since today was a special occasion. Or so I thought. *What a pity.*

"Hey Eve, are you okay? You were gone for quite a while. Your food got cold." Oli grabs a tissue for me.

"Everything is fine. Thank you for your concern." I barely have the courage to speak.

My appetite is completely gone, but I try my best not to make things awkward by not eating my food. My mom taught me to never waste food. Especially since there are people around the world who are starving. We silently munch on our meals. All the while, I feel extremely awkward, and the confidence I'd felt before the museum seems to have gone down the drain in the bathroom.

CHAPTER 10

I say a short prayer, "Lord, please guide me during these tough times. You will put people into my life who need to be there. I trust that you will always love me and be my guide. In Jesus' name, amen."

It's 6:00 p.m. I head over to Cockle Bay to somehow make myself feel better. Nature has a way of doing that. The breeze feels so good on my skin as I breathe the fresh air in and out. Over the ledge, I peer at the bay, which creates a breathtaking illusion. Blue, green, yellow, and red lights up the water, mirroring the skyscrapers. During this time of year, Sydney is chilly, whereas in the States, it would be scorching hot even when the sun goes down.

No one is around since it's a weekday. That's probably for the best because I need to be alone right now. I hear the loud sound of rushing water and follow it out of curiosity. A beautiful water fountain with bird statues surrounding it that appear to be dancing sits in the center of a walkway. *How cute.*

All of a sudden, an older couple comes out of nowhere with a large boombox. They take each other's hands and begin shaking to the music. At first, it seems kind of slow and boring.

But then, the music changes from salsa to a mix of hip-hop and pop. The drums force my hips to start moving on their own. Other people begin showing up and immediately join in. All the diversity that's been hiding this whole time has suddenly appeared, and I feel my sadness washing away.

I get up and wipe my face dry to do what I know best—dance. Pretending no one is watching, I shake my hips round and round to the beat. I raise my hands above my head, feeling the motion moving left and right.

The crowd becomes huge. Where did they come from? Everyone is dancing without a care in the world, as if this is a normal occurrence. From a distance, I can see a couple arguing. The man invites his lover to dance, making her face light up. Even a little kid dances like a robot next to me.

There is so much power in dancing. It's one thing that all people have in common: the inability to resist good music. I completely forgot about the situation with Oli. It shouldn't matter so much to me whether he has a girlfriend or not. We literally just met. Although it would have been nice to get to know him better. Maybe we can just be friends?

My mom put me in dance classes from the moment I could walk. Dancing salsa in Cuban culture is huge. Although ballet was way too slow for my liking, my absolute favorite type of dance is hip-hop. The beats allow me to let myself go. It got me through the nights of crying after Lucas hit me or shamed me by using bugs to his advantage.

My throat is completely dry. I'm having so much fun right now. Dance allows me to be in my element without feeling shame. My dance teacher once told me that the way we dance is an art in itself. It's also super contagious. There are about thirty people shaking their bodies to the beats. Seeing everyone enjoying this makes me smile.

~

THE NEXT MORNING, staying in and being comforted the rest of the week feels like a tempting option. Still, there are only a few more days left in Australia. I can mope around or enjoy the rest of my time here since the trip wasn't cheap.

Every day here feels like a treasured gem, while back home, a week often drags on endlessly. I wonder if this will be my fate when I officially retire. No sense of urgency for any reason, being able to wake up at any time of the day, and eating meals without anxiety or pressure. The opportunities will be endless. But my parents don't seem to enjoy being older. Now that they have all the time in the world, finding something to do to keep busy gets more and more difficult by the day. My dad can sit on the couch watching random shows all day long while Mom does her best to maintain all the decades' worth of hobbies she has accumulated. Good on her for trying. Most people give up after hobbies become too hard or boring.

Google helps me decide which café still serves a mid-morning breakfast. The lobby has free breakfast, but it doesn't help when I keep waking up late. With only thirty minutes before noon, I trot out of the hotel. A nice breeze cools me down. I walk in silence, admiring the atmosphere and the genuine beauty of every small mom-and-pop shop I pass by. There are bookstores, bars, and different secret spots to view the ocean. The sun beams on my head, making a migraine imminent. It gets the best of me, forcing my legs to slow down.

I find a bench completely empty, awaiting my arrival. A tree had been perfectly placed nearby to provide a sufficient amount of shade. It is exactly what I need. Suddenly, I feel something touch me. I try not to freak out because it's probably my imagination. My mind must be playing tricks on me. But then, the tickle intensifies, forcing me to look down to scratch the spot.

"Ack!" *Why me?* I get up and start shaking myself off in disgust and agony.

A giant spider flings to the floor, staying put as if nothing happened. *Seriously?* That thing has no shame.

I take a close look at the creature. Its body is light brown with eight flawless yet hairy legs. It has two pinchers in the front close to its head. The butt on that thing is large and fat. I've never seen such a big spider in my entire life. It gives me the creeps.

According to Google, some individuals in Australia like to keep tarantulas as pets and then release them when they get way too big. They roam around endlessly, looking for their owners. It could be that I reminded the spider of its owner. *Yuck.* I would never willingly have a pet spider in my home. What if it gets out of its enclosure and turns me into food?

The café is very pleasant with plant life everywhere. The owner seems to be a huge fan of moss and cat portraits. I aim to get a matcha bubble tea and a grilled cheese sandwich. It appears the café does not sell any breakfast food since I'm too late.

One of the cat paintings reminds me of a fatter version of Garfield. Someday, I'd love to paint like that. It's clear that the artist put their heart and soul into it. The strokes of the paintbrush are so perfectly planned. That's the thing about art and a good lesson in life: it doesn't have to be perfect all the time. My parents taught me while I was in high school to stay away from no-good boys, who aim for only one thing. My mom did not want me to make the same mistakes she had made when she was sixteen, living in America for the first time. She went out with boys who wanted to marry her, but left each time things started to get serious. Until she met the person of her dreams– my dad. He was a player, not even giving my mom a glance during their years of schooling together. It wasn't until one day that they ended up at the same beach when a shark attack happened. People ran for their lives while my parents stayed at the beach to make sure everyone was safe. They bonded over the fact that all their friends were cowards. Weird story, but one thing led to the next, and I was born. It's amazing to find out where life can lead you by just going with the flow and accepting possibilities.

"Hey Eve, fancy seeing you here." Oli walks up with a beautiful girl attached to his bicep.

Oh no. I'm not ready.

CHAPTER 11

"Oh, hey!" I say in a mellow tone.

"I'd like to introduce you to my girlfriend, Amelia," Oli says with all the excitement in the world. I'm glad he didn't bring up anything about yesterday.

My heart hasn't had enough time to recover from the news that his heart has been taken by another woman. It's very clear that he's extremely proud of her. She's beautiful, after all. Strawberry blond curls with cute bangs. Even her outfit would be impossible to copy because it's too unique.

"Oli told me that you love bugs! I was so excited to meet you. It seems like he and I are the only two people on the face of the planet who share that specific interest!" Amelia says with a huge smile on her face.

Wait, what? He told her I "love bugs". That's not the case. It was all a false impression to get to know him better. Then again, I did act like I was enjoying yesterday, looking at all those disgusting things with passion. The truth is, I was simply ecstatic to be in the presence of a gorgeous person who could help me conquer my fear.

"Yep, that's right," I respond.

"Well, we need to hang out and chat! Do you mind if we sit with you?"

Oh no. I don't know what to say. I freeze in utter silence while my brain comes up with a fight-or-flight plan. They sit down, inviting themselves. *Help me.* I look down at my hands in a panic, not knowing what to do with them.

"So, where are you from? You're obviously not from around here."

Offended, I don't know how to respond. Racism could be rampant here for all I know; maybe it's my olive skin color or even my hair texture being wavy and flamboyant. Amelia notices my discomfort and parts her lips in a tiny gasp.

"Oh no, no, please take no offense. I'm merely referring to your accent. It's very cute!"

Oli breaks the ice by telling her how we met and that we went to the museum to study more about bugs. She gets on my nerves. I'm not usually one to judge, but man, she is annoying. Amelia is the type of person who cannot hold a proper conversation without offending someone. Instantly, I dislike her for the fact that she stole the heart of that amazing guy. They talk and laugh together so fluently as if they've known each other their entire lives.

"So, Eve, why don't we all go to a park together? Amelia and I were planning on going to Cooper Park when we decided to get a bite to eat," he mentions with those beautiful hazel eyes. How could I say no to him?

"Sure, I'd love to!" I respond without thinking. It would be the perfect opportunity to get to know people who have a deep passion for insects. Something like that is unheard of in Miami. Seeing them together might help me move on, I pray.

We walk out of the café together in utter awkwardness. Oli seems to be the only one having a blast. That man can make any moment good even when all fails. The two of them stride up front, leading the way, while I stay back slightly.

Amelia comes to the back, bombarding me with questions. "Eve, so tell me, what are your hobbies? I would love to get to know you more and be here for you these next few days," she says cheerfully.

"Oh, okay, sure. I like swimming at the beach, and by swimming, I mean doggy paddling my way in the shallow children's section of a lagoon." I laugh at my own joke.

"Ha, you are too funny. I do the same thing! Oli is constantly having to drag me into the deep end of the water, but I'm always screaming for him to bring me back. Short people like us can't take those risks! What if there's a shark?!"

"You're not wrong." I laugh with her. "Another hobby I have is dancing, but I stopped doing it after my parents couldn't afford to keep sending me to classes."

"Oh, you have to show me some moves!"

I rub my left forearm while looking down at the ground. "Oh, I don't know. You see, I'm a little rusty."

"Don't be so modest. Let's go to a street dance party sometime."

For some reason, I have a feeling that she's actually genuine. I need more friends like her. It's clear why Oli is so happy being with Amelia. She's got a charm that could make any sad person smile. I start to think maybe I've been too judgy and was just upset that Oli's taken.

"Hey Amelia? How did you and Oli meet?" I ask.

"We've been together for as long as I can remember. I have pictures of us taking a bath together as babies because our parents were best friends," she continues. "For a few years, we didn't get along because he wanted to go on a date with me so badly. I ended up dating other people and getting hurt. You know what? Oli has always been there to pick me up. I couldn't get rid of him, and now I'm marrying him. It's funny how life likes to play tricks on you. You think your life is going to end up a certain way, but then it takes a turn towards something even better."

"I wonder if I'll ever find the right one."

"Someday, Eve, you'll find your one. Be open minded at all times. It will happen when you're not looking."

"Everyone here in Sydney is super friendly, huh?" I ask.

"Definitely. We try our best to make everyone feel at home. It's an extremely busy place with a lot of young adults doing crazy things. We try to prevent that by being welcoming," Amelia responds.

Oli sees that we have fallen super far behind.

"Hey, you two! Hurry, we're getting close to the park," he yells to get our attention.

"Coming!" we shout back at the same time. "Ditto!" Simultaneously, we giggle.

CHAPTER 12

*A*t the front of the entrance, we sit down on the curb to take a breather from all the walking. It's also a great opportunity to take a look at the giant map so we don't end up getting lost. Sweat is dripping all over my body, even though the walk was only twenty minutes from the café. I've always felt self-conscious about the smell of my armpits. I've tried many different types of deodorants in my life, all to end up with one that does not work or blocks sweat pores so much that it causes little lumps. For some reason, the right side always tends to be smellier than the left, so I end up putting extra deodorant on that side. Then there's the scary talk about cancer if you use too much. Winning is impossible. There have been times when I go to the store, and there's a random stranger who smells like straight-up B.O. The whole aisle smells putrid, but the feelings of guilt start to well up when I don't have the courage to confess it to the person.

No one seems to notice or mind whether I smell or don't smell here. So why am I consistently freaking out over this?

The first bug we see is vibrant with yellow and black patterns. It's huge, with red-bugged eyes popping out of its head. Mating season for insects can happen throughout the year if the temperature is right. Most wait till either spring or summer. The creature stays put as Oli moves close enough to point his camera in its direction. I can hear the sound of the lens adjusting for perfect lighting, then going completely silent. Oli has his shutter off to make sure not to scare the creature away. Success. Amelia watches him lovingly and in awe as he smiles with much pride.

"Guys, come and take a closer look. This bug is called a cicada. They're one of the largest insects in Sydney and the most beloved creatures," he continues. "They like to suck on sap, and when they lay eggs, it can take up to seventeen years to emerge. Birds love to munch on them if they can be caught."

Amelia's deep in nerd-mode with Oli but finally spots my confusion and begins to explain. "Oli grew up spending a lot of time alone. His parents had to be at work all the time since they were—and still are—lead biologists. The majority of his early childhood was spent with me since my mum babysat him daily. We played outside with mud and bugs like every other kid. We would trap bugs in containers at times and keep them until they needed to be released," she adds. "Did you ever do anything similar growing up?"

"I did not. A horrible human being ruined any good experience I could ever have with insects. He used my fear against me and put them inside my clothes. He would also squish their guts and force me to eat them when the teachers weren't around. No one did a thing to help me," I mention reluctantly, yet I feel that Oli and Amelia can be trusted.

"Oh… I'm so very sorry to hear that. I didn't realize you were afraid. We didn't have a situation like that, per se, but going to school was very hard in Sydney for our generation. You either make it, or you don't. Bugs were our only way of getting away from the high expectations of everyone else, hence why we're studying it." Amelia frowns, holding onto her arms for comfort. "If it helps, my dad was never part of the picture. For a few years, I received a few gifts from an anonymous sender that I assumed was him. But then, they eventually stopped. It hurts sometimes to think about it, but I stopped hoping for him to return since he didn't bother trying to get to know me. My mum was more than enough for me, and I had Oli."

Amelia and I hug because no other words can be said to help the situation. Life is hard, but at least we have other people in our lives to help us through it. Being in nature can bring feelings out effectively. It's one thing that I get to do back home each time I go to the beach. Problems can be left behind when swimming in the water. I've heard that people sometimes climb mountains to scream out all of their frustrations as a form of release. It's one of my goals to try it out someday. I'd probably scream, "I hate Lucas!" at the top of my lungs.

"I want to teach you a trick." Amelia begins to untie her shoelaces, then removes both shoes along with the socks. "I know this looks crazy, but please try it out."

It can't hurt to try it, although I completely forgot to paint my toenails. *How embarrassing!* My feet are gross. No one peeks down to look except for me. It makes me feel better that Amelia also has unpainted and unattended toenails. Though I'm still unsure why we're even taking our shoes off.

"When you walk the forest barefoot, it produces a wave of feeling grounded to nature." She walks slowly, teaching me the correct pace. "Our feet have senses that are distorted by the shoes we wear."

"Wow, that's amazing. I used to do this as a kid until I squashed a beetle that was sitting in the driveway," I mention, getting chills from that horrible memory.

"It's a natural massage that can strengthen your foot muscles, which can benefit your posture, along with improving mental health."

The ground is freezing cold. What a nice break from the afternoon heat. I scan the dirt with the fear of stepping on a rusty nail. A hospital trip definitely isn't part of the plan. Each step sends a tickling sensation up my leg. The forest is beautiful, with ferns all around and trees that have roots that are ancient. We hold hands tightly, descending the staircase that lacks a railing. Luckily, the moss shields our feet from the cracks embedded into the concrete.

Stopping at a mini waterfall, the crisp scent carries a hint of wet stone and a metallic undertone. Oli remains in his own little world, looking for more bugs to take a picture of. He's doing research for a term paper that's due by the end of the month. Amelia goes to the same college, but they decided that taking different courses would make the process more fun. Without shoes, the time seems much slower. Walking feels more intentional as every step is calculated.

Amelia excitedly takes a step into the pond, feeling the sharp but not deadly rocks on her heel. Curiously, I follow her into the freezing cold water. The stream moves with the wind in a motion that is therapeutic. All the stress that I suffered yesterday melts away. Small fish in the water come searching for food, getting super close to our feet. I take a deep breath in and let it out. *I can do this. They aren't going to bite my toes off. Or are they?*

"Over there! I see something!" Oli yells.

It startles both of us, but we remain calm, understanding that one wrong move can cut the bottoms of our feet. I take hold of a nearby, sturdy tree branch to balance out of the pond safely, helping Amelia back to the lush grass. My feet feel tingly, like getting out of a warm bathtub.

On the other side of the same tree, a little green-speckled bug, similar to a dragonfly, appears. Its wings resemble a net, almost lacy. The eyes are golden and metallic looking. With such confidence, it's unafraid of our presence. What brilliance.

"These are called lacewings. They are the type of critter that any good farmer wants in their vegetable garden," Oli speaks in awe of such a specimen as if he had found gold.

"What makes them so special?" I ask, genuinely curious.

"They eat the pesky critters that destroy vegetables," Amelia responds.

I put my shoes back on to enjoy the rest of the way without worrying about stepping on anything. I never knew that there were good bugs and bad bugs. I always just assumed that they were all bad, disgusting creatures that bite and chase humans for no good reason.

"Thank you so much for inviting me on this super cool adventure. I learned so much. I really needed this," I explain to Oli and Amelia.

"Oh sure, no problem. I'm not sure when you'll be back in Sydney, but let's do this again sometime," Oli says hopefully, with Amelia bobbing her head in agreement.

"You bet!"

CHAPTER 13

tour guide isn't needed since Sydney is a civilized place to be. The city is very similar to Miami, especially with the number of things to do here. I feel safe enough to walk the streets on my own using the GPS on my phone. Deciding on food is easier than ever based on what I'm craving; it can be typed into the search bar of Google, where hundreds of options will be displayed. It doesn't help that I unintentionally always pick fast food to save a buck.

There are so many different options to choose from, like going on a romantic pirate ship dinner or ziplining across the Blue Mountains. I decide to go bold with a fancy helicopter ride that departs in two hours, not nearly enough time to pick a decent outfit. Tight jeans wouldn't be wise, but short shorts have never been my forte. I don't necessarily like it when people stare at my skinny chicken legs. When I was little, Mom used to urge me to eat more so that my legs wouldn't break when I ran at school. Forcing myself to eat never worked out. In Cuban culture, being too skinny is considered distasteful. Having more weight meant being in a good financial position. It's a status-based hierarchy. Although my grandma always made a point that I was perfectly fine the way I was.

The plane ride ends up being super cheap for a private ride. Starting from Kingsford Smith Airport, I meet the pilots who already have their headgear and uniforms on. Pilots always remind me of military video games like Call of Duty. Their faces are barely visible, making me wonder if there's an alien beneath that fancy suit.

The engine rumbles loudly enough that no one has to interact socially. It's exactly what I need. Time at peace to think. However, too much of it can be a problem sometimes. In my apartment, I think about being stuck in the same situation for eternity, how I might end up single and alone forever. With all the self-doubt each day, it was hard to get out of bed with any motivation to move my feet and go to work. Giving myself pep talks in the morning was the only escape from that kind of thinking. Music played a strong role. I would play it loud enough for the neighbors to bang on their roof. I didn't care if people were sleeping. Dancing to loud, catchy pop music uplifted me.

Tall, clean buildings are everywhere in sight. The sun beams at shiny buildings, making them sparkle and glisten. The bay is nothing short of magical. Boats cruise along its waves, completely nonchalant about the world. Even kayaks can be seen from up above, paddling super close to other, much larger boats. I haven't been kayaking before, mostly because of the fear of falling into the water where there are alligators waiting for their prey. South Florida has had an alligator problem for years. People release random reptiles into the wild without caring about the consequences. Animals in unnatural habitats end up causing huge problems and overrule the animals that are supposed to be living there, causing them to flee or die.

Oh wow. I'm in complete awe as the helicopter swoops over the ocean. The beaches have sand that's pure and golden brown, the color of brown sugar. There's no trash whatsoever, not like in Miami. The city is flawless and very well maintained. I wonder if high taxes are charged to keep up with this beauty.

The pilot finally speaks up, "Do you see something poking out of the water?"

It's very hard to see from so high up, but after squinting in place with one eye closed, there it is—a big, beautiful, majestic giant fish dancing in the water for attention. It shows its white belly with tons of pride. *How adorable.* It's so sad to think that back in the seventeenth century, whales were hunted and slaughtered for their blubber. With it, bar soaps were made until hydrogenation was invented, replacing the cruel whale-killing method. People didn't seem to like the strong odor of the blubber anyway.

She looks so majestic, going in and out of the water like it's her hobby. The copilot takes out his phone to snap a picture before the moment ends. I didn't think of doing so for fear of missing out on such a beautiful sight. I always get blinded when something important is happening. After my grandpa died at the early age of sixty, it hurt so much not being next to him. He used to make me laugh by taking his dentures out and making a strange sound like a monster. Cancer hit him hard, leaving my grandma all alone. They were married for almost forty years, paving the way for my father to make it to the United States. When he passed away, I felt the reality that life is short, something that I knew but didn't quite fully understand.

Believing in Jesus is a guarantee of salvation. Knowing that I have a secure spot in heaven makes living a little more comfortable. Even if this helicopter were to face engine failure, I know that I would be all right.

The blue helicopter lands peacefully on the circular pad with crew chiefs awaiting our safe return. The pilots shake my hand and tell me that it has been an honor flying together. It was definitely worth the money. Such a thrilling twenty-minute experience. From afar, I see a large green truck coming to refuel the aircraft. It's amusing to watch the mechanics work diligently as if it were their baby. They are so focused and dedicated.

Hunger begins to kick in as I watch all these guys working hard. I have never been good at choosing what to eat. If the decision were always left to me, I'd be having eggs with spam for every meal. Those are the easiest things on my recipe list that don't require too much thinking or effort. Ramen is the second choice. It's easy to pop that thing into a boiling pot of water for four minutes, slurp on noodles, and enjoy the delightful soup that soothes the soul. Cooking isn't my specialty, but it's needed to survive in this world. Going out to eat can be time-consuming. Not to mention expensive.

For some reason, the word *seafood* pops into my brain.

Arriving at a small mom-and-pop grill, the waitress chooses the best spot in the restaurant for me, near the window with a gorgeous view of the garden. Everything is intentionally placed a certain way to make the magic happen. Red tulips stare me in the face with such magnificence. Yellow tulips are placed directly in the middle of the garden in a small circle, creating an aerial view of a large red flower. Bushes have been placed on the sides, creating leaves. *Such a work of art.* Who came up with such a smart idea? Only someone skilled in horticulture.

"Hello mate, what can I get for you?" the waitress asks. I haven't had a chance to look over the menu since the beauty of the garden placed me in a daze.

"I'll take whatever the chef recommends," I boldly proclaim.

"Of course, it comes with bread on the side. Is that okay?"

"Absolutely, bread would be lovely."

"Okay, got it. I figured I'd ask because most people are on special diets these days."

"Oh, not me. Thanks for letting me choose."

"Of course. I'll be right back with your dish. Give us a few minutes."

The reviews of this little grill range from four to five stars. It's easy to see why. Many people are dining in today. There's nothing like sitting in a restaurant, smelling the food, and getting the full experience and ambience. Back home, I normally get food to go since the traffic is unbearable past 3:00 p.m. Once you go into the abyss of vehicles, there's no getting out for a couple of hours. It's nice to take a break from such a massive city.

The same waitress comes out shortly after with a giant plate of some unknown meat for the table next to me. Smells of butter fill the room, inspiring me to try to cook a nice meal after I get back home. My heart fills with delight as I watch the man take his first bite with the satisfying look that the food tastes amazing. But then, I look closely to see that the mysterious meat is something I've never seen in my life before. Its head has polka dots with the eyes carved out. Its arms are a beautiful yellow and brown color. *Oh no.* I stop myself from looking after I realize what the creature is—a sea turtle.

With little time to think, the waitress shortly comes to deliver plates to my table. I completely forgot about what I just saw, as the smell of the food is mesmerizing. Plus, it's rude to stare and to judge someone else's taste.

"This is a three-course meal, enjoy!" The waitress leaves looking satisfied.

The chef comes out to greet me, pleased to have the power to make the decision on my meal. "It's an honor to serve you. Please save all questions for the end of the meal for the greatest experience with different types of delicacies."

Moment of truth. I take my very first bite of the first dish. The bread is scrumptious with a hint of rosemary and olive oil. Unsure what any of the meats are, I am feeling super adventurous today. Traveling makes it easier to become an open-minded person, increasing the chances of cool and unplanned opportunities. The smell of butter and lemon fills the air with a delicious fragrance.

The first meat is slightly chewy, a combination of chicken and veal. Silkiness melts in my mouth. *Oh wow. This is delicious!* The stewed tomatoes pair perfectly with the meat. I feel greedy eating such high-class food. My parents would have loved this. Especially my dad; he'd literally eat anything that moves if he could. When he lived in Cuba, food options were not a thing. The general public was awarded rations of food depending on how many people were in the family. Things like rice, beans, chicken, eggs, and a few fish were all that were given. Pork and beef had to be requested and approved by the government.

Dad told me once that he's afraid of going back to a system like that. Forced to go to the military at a young age, rumors of a civil war were terrifying since he didn't have a choice but to work for the government. Mom had a slightly better experience since she was lucky enough to live on her grandparents' farm. They had an abundance of animals and vegetables as long as the proper ration was given to government authorities once per week. If they had refused to do so, they'd be punished. I am very fortunate to have been born in a good country.

The next dish entails a buttery, creamy soup with specks of basil floating around. The carrots and baby corn are the sweetest things I've ever tasted. The meat is white, soft, and very chewy. It has to be a cousin in the lobster family. It also came with a side of salad with massive raw shrimp on top. Unfortunately, the eyes and the head still being attached are a huge turn-off for me. I do not like being looked at by the creature I'm currently ingesting. Although it's a friendly reminder that it was once a living thing that got taken from its home to be eaten.

The waitress comes right over to see how I'm doing. "Is everything okay? Do you need anything else? Are you ready for the last dish?"

"Oh yes, more than ready. This is the best seafood I've ever had in my entire existence. Thank you so much," I say. If only this moment would never end. It's hard to come by seafood that's cooked this good.

I sip some water to see if that'll help the food go down more effectively. It doesn't. My tummy only gets bigger, making it hard to think of eating anything additional. Is it too late to say no? A mountain of mango ice cream sitting on a bed of kiwi and strawberries comes my way. One bite, and I instantly notice how the coconut balances the natural flavors of everything. Even the mango ice cream is completely natural, with no added sugars. The chef truly outdid himself with this wonderful meal. The waitress asks if I'd like chocolate drizzled on top, but I find that it's not truly necessary. Ice cream has always been my favorite, especially after a long day at work.

I pay my bill, graciously awaiting the chef to come out as he promised. I'd like to ask what the mystery meat was and thank him for all that he does. The man has raw talent. I am pleased to have experienced such a meal. I'll have to come here again in the future with Sarah. She'd absolutely love it here.

"How did you like the food? Do you have any questions?" the chef asks.

"I'm sure you heard me say it to Gabi, the waitress, but all I can say is wow. This was the best seafood I've ever had in my life. I have to ask, what was that mysterious meat? I couldn't put my finger on what it could have been."

"Ah, yes. What you have eaten is a delicacy from an island in Australia called Tasmania. My family and I love to share the cuisine since it is so rare." The chef continues, "Sea turtles are part of our culture. Under the Native Title Act, we are able to produce these delicious dishes sparingly."

My jaw drops. I can feel my heart beating fast. The thought of having eaten a sea turtle makes me very sad. Yet, I am happy to have experienced the delicacy once in my lifetime. Respectfully, I thank the chef.

CHAPTER 14

*C*entral Station has the fastest-paced system I've ever seen. I've only been on a train once, when I was in middle school. My dad craved White Castle; I mean the real one, not the ones from the freezer section at Walmart. The issue was that the best way to get there was by the Metrorail. Parking can be impossible in certain parts of Miami. It smelled like rusting metal and stinky feet. The smell comes back to me any time I hear the mention of getting onto a train. I stayed as close as I could to my mom in fear of getting shoved out the window. There were no seatbelts or seats available anyway. We were forced to squeeze in with many other people trying to go shopping or get back home.

Good thing I thought of inviting Oli and Amelia to go on this trip with me. Departing alone would be less fun. Plus, they can be my guide in a different city to find the famous three sisters in the Blue Mountains. It's a three-hour ride that I wouldn't want to spend in my own thoughts. Being around those two uplifts my soul even when the memories of Lucas hurt me and fog up my brain.

This train has perfectly good seats to sit on. Passengers do not have to hold on for dear life. I'm seriously in shock. It's not what I'm used to in Miami. Even the train station is an easy process to follow. Walking in, there are signs everywhere pointing to the ticketing booth. The ticket master points us in the direction of the train to get on. I have a bit of a scare since we arrived quite late, and the train leaves as soon as we have our tickets in hand. Feelings of hopelessness overwhelm me. All tickets are nonrefundable. I ran to the conductor, explaining the situation, almost in tears. He laughs at me like I'm being ridiculous. Oli and Amelia try to stop me, but I don't listen.

"No, no, mate. Not to worry," he asserts. "All tickets are meant to be used once at any time of the day."

"Oh! Thank you so much, sir!" I exclaim.

"Not a problem. Here's the next one coming now."

We quickly climb on as soon as the conductor shouts, "All aboard!" not wanting to get left behind a second time. The conductor is so kind. He must have known that I was a tourist. What an embarrassment. But there's no time to even think about it. The last thing I want on this trip is to get lost at a train station.

The scenery immediately changes from the city to beautiful nature. The town of Katoomba has such a romantic charm. After getting off the luxurious train, a designated bus takes us to our first stop, the Echo Point Lookout. We walk up a flight of stairs that's going to take so much longer than it should because of the number of other tourists who have the same idea. I never expected this many people to be here on a weekday. Then again, it is summer vacation. The ravine is dazzling with forests and sandstone ridges. The natural beauty of the craggy cliffs is captured in the background of our abundance of selfies.

"Hey, Eve, let's get closer to those people over there. It looks like there's a tour being given. We can just listen to what he's saying," Amelia whispers.

Heading in the direction to the right, there is indeed a guy giving a tour of the Blue Mountains. He explains that they got their name due to the mountains being actually blue because of the eucalyptus oil droplets from the trees, lots of dust, and water vapor. These mountains are ancient, about 300 million years old, which is even older than the Grand Canyon. Apparently, there is proof that the descendants of ancient human species, or Aboriginals, once inhabited the area, as there are rock carvings and art in certain parts of the mountains. The tour guide begins eyeballing us. It's so awkward that we walk in a different direction, pretending that we weren't listening to his story. I don't want him to think we're some kind of freeloaders.

A small hike leads the way to see "The Sisters". The Triplets are famous and even have a specific legend. The air smells fresh, exactly what I need to let go of stress. The path is very well-paved. I don't see any light poles indicating that we needed to get the ball rolling. Fear of being out at night has been beaten into me from watching all the scary movies, especially during Halloween. As a family, we did not care for the holiday except for the candy that was half price the day after. My favorite candies were all the chocolates, especially Baby Ruth. Its nutty, caramel, chocolatey goodness was hard to resist. Although I went to the dentist once a year, I got into a lot of trouble having many cavities develop. At the time, dental insurance pricing was quite high, but my dad always wanted me to smile brightly with good teeth. It was a luxury that he never had in his home country.

The thought of getting captured by random people living in the mountains does terrify me.

"Lord God, please keep us safe. We are in a territory in which we do not know what's out there. Our sense of adventure is saying go, while fear is saying no. Give us the strength to keep moving forward. In the name of the mighty Lord Jesus, amen," I pray.

The honeymoon bridge arrives instantly. I was concerned

for no reason. The rock formation is unbelievable. How can patterns like this be formed naturally? The height can be frightening when looking down. The story of the three sisters taking the unusual rock formation is quite odd. Their names are Gunnedoo, Meehni, and Wimlah. The three lovely ladies had fallen madly in love with three brothers who were from the neighboring town, but unfortunately, marriage was forbidden. Pissed off at the tribes' decision to restrict their love, the brothers captured the three sisters in order to marry them in their own tribe. A war broke out to save the three sisters when a local Katoomba elder placed a strong spell, turning the sisters into stone. The spell failed to be reversed since the elder ended up dying in the midst of all the chaos. What a scary story. It's so unfair that the sisters had to pay for someone else's bad decisions. That tribe shouldn't have had any power over them.

Time goes by at razor-sharp speed, forcing us to walk to the bus stop in silence. One awaits our arrival with perfect timing. There's something reassuring about the bus's familiar presence. As we board, I notice that the bus isn't nearly as packed as earlier this morning.

"Wow, that story was quite dark, huh?" Amelia sighs.

"Yes, it was so sad. I hope that my parents never restrict me from being in love," I respond.

"Just tell them how you feel. Your parents would understand."

"Eh, it depends."

The bus suddenly stops, and we embark on the Skyway East Station. The entrance is beautiful. Everyone around us looks extremely happy to be there. It reminds me of going to amusement parks with butterflies in my stomach each time I go on any of the rides. We board the scenic railway, an enclosed train that goes four meters per second. Apparently, there's a very steep incline at about fifty-two degrees. If I end up throwing up, I'll try my best to continue moving forward. This is a once-in-a-lifetime thing. We choose the laidback version, adjusting the originally seated position so that everything can be seen.

The railway descends fast into the mouth of a cliff. I look over to my left and right, but I can't see Oli or Amelia, who are sitting right next to me. Instead, all I hear are terrifying screams as if we are about to be engulfed. The darkness lasts only a few seconds, but in the moment, it feels like a million years. My life flashes before my eyes when the light suddenly appears, and the railway begins slowing down to a stop.

We all laugh at the fact that I screamed at the top of my lungs as if I were about to die or something. Oli mimics the face I made when the light finally showed up. Normally, I wouldn't be interested in a ride so strenuous.

"Your hair slapped me in the face!" Amelia says, handing me a hair tie.

"I'm so sorry. I forgot to put it up. I didn't think this ride was going to shake me that much. That was terrifying!" I exclaim.

"Wanna go again? It'll be fun," Oli tempts.

"No. I'm good. Once was more than enough."

My hair always tends to get on other people. I shed more than our family dog. Follicles end up all over the floor, on jackets, pillowcases, blankets, and even sometimes my own food. *Gross.* Sarah's mom once mentioned that my hair stayed in their house for weeks after I came to visit them. I believed it since I'm the only one with dark, wavy hair. Her family has blond, luscious, straight hair that looks perfectly brushed even after sleeping for twelve hours straight and rolling around the bed. Sarah wishes she had dark, wavy hair, while I wish I had blond, straight hair. Why is that thing? Humans always want what they don't have.

Even children found the ride amazing. Before getting off, I peek over to see a little girl, probably the age of four, asking her daddy to go on it again. She's so brave. When I was her age, my mom always tried to keep me safe from doing anything too strenuous. She wanted to take good care of me. I'm very thankful for her. I didn't mind not doing the things other kids were doing until I became a grumpy, stressed-out teenager. Pimples, periods, and boys were a few of my worries.

The next stop is the scenic Skyway. About eighty-four passengers can squish into it. My neck feels itchy, thinking that someone might rock the cable car. We find a spot inside closest to a window near the front to view the mountains perfectly. However, a couple of people get upset about not getting first dibs. *You snooze, you lose.* The gorgeous ravine truly does look blue in the distance.

"Oh, my goodness, look!" I exclaim, pointing towards the lookout area where there's a group of teenagers hanging from the railing.

"What in the world are they doing?!" Amelia responds, terrified.

Onlookers watch them in disbelief, shaking their heads at the boys who are unaware of the danger they are putting themselves in. Other people in the Skyway point towards the kids, taking videos just in case they decide to jump. Why would anyone take a video of this?! Those boys truly don't have any fear of falling. Moments like this can turn tragic at the least expected time. But no one does anything about it.

We fly past them after moments of terror. I do not want to see anything go wrong. The views we have seen are remarkable. I never would have imagined that anything like this would be found in Australia. I always thought it was a complete and utter desert. The Blue Mountains have their own rainforest. The air feels moist, making my hair poof up. It doesn't matter since I am super comfortable being here with Oli and Amelia.

My parents decided only to have me for financial reasons. Even though I begged for a sibling, my mom would tell me that it wasn't practical. Children are very expensive, always needing to buy clothes, always hungry, and always wanting the next best thing. I knew from the beginning that they were always working hard to make ends meet. They did a fabulous job until they were able to retire and kindly kicked me out of their house. Dad performed engineering work at the local power factory. As far as I knew, it was hard labor that required his mind and soul. Even after coming home every day exhausted, he still made enough time for Mom and me.

Another flight of stairs. *Oh no.* I've had enough walking for one day. But it is the only way to descend back to the bus stop, which will take us back to the train station. My stomach bubbles up from the snack I ate an hour ago. I start to struggle to move fast enough.

"Hey Eve, will you be available tomorrow?" Oli asks.

"Of course, why? What's going on?" I respond, hoping I'll see them tomorrow.

"We've got a surprise for you, hehe. Please say you'll come?" Amelia jumps in.

"Oh, all right. I can't say no to you guys. Tell me where to go and I'll be there."

IN A TRANCE after getting back to my hotel room, my eyes fail me.

I am at a wedding on the beach. The music is obnoxiously loud but catchy and so loving. Her father, Amelia's father, holds her arm as they both make their way to the altar. They give each other a loving gaze. His eyes say, "I'm so blessed to be here with you on the most important day of your life." Oliver stands up there, awaiting his beloved wife. They hold each other as if they couldn't live without one another. Then, my mouth randomly begins to move without my consent. Everyone stops talking to beam at me. *How embarrassing. I hate being the center of attention.*

"What do you mean you object, Eve? Is there something you

want to say?" Oliver says with an angry tone I've never heard come out of his mouth.

Suddenly, I become a monster, trying to destroy something beautiful. All the hatred buried away in my heart comes out at Oliver, the groom, the one that I had a small crush on only a few days ago. Everyone can't believe their ears. I hear gasps all around me. Even the person next to me gives me an evil, dirty look. All the blue and green gorgeous eyes of his and her family beam at me with hate.

"I understand that's how you feel. But I only met you a few days ago. The real love of my life is this beautiful woman standing before me." Oliver looks into Amelia's eyes, tipping her chin up. "I adore you, Amelia. Always have, always will."

They kiss, but not one of those traditional embarrassing wedding kisses that are seen in movies. The kiss is intimate, loving, and with tongues and saliva all over the place. I don't even have time to watch because, at that moment, I'm grabbed by Oliver's brute of an uncle, who is actually the chef at the restaurant yesterday.

"You're the one who cooked me the delicious meal. Don't tell me Oliver eats sea turtles, too?!" I demand.

"He eats all the sea turtles I cook, just so you know." He lets out an evil laugh.

"No!" I yell in agony.

I wake up drenched in sweat. Literally swimming in the bed. It's midnight. *What just happened?* Waking up from a nightmare can be terrifying. Especially not knowing what's reality, and what isn't. The feeling of guilt haunts my soul. How could I have ruined such a perfect moment like that? What in the world is wrong with me? I have to tell him the truth.

CHAPTER 15

*J*hear loud music playing. It's extremely tempting to bob my head to the beat, but Amelia is holding her hand over my eyes for the surprise. A smile breaks out over my face because I can vaguely see through the cracks of her fingers. Being slightly shorter than everyone else has its pros and cons. In this case, as we move forward, her fingers begin to get tired.

"Surprise!" Amelia and Oli say simultaneously.

My mouth opens wide. I'm in awe. Multiple people are gathered together, dancing silly to the music. One person is break dancing while another is holding their spouse close and slow dancing. Grandmas and grandpas are doing the boogie. My cheeks redden at the thought of these two doing all of this for me. No one has ever been this kind.

"How did you... Pull this off?" I ask in deep reverence.

"Well, you mentioned that you enjoy dancing. We wanted to show you what it's like to street dance in Sydney. Plus, I'll have to take you up on that promise to show me some moves," Amelia responds giddily.

"Earlier, we brought out a sign that said, 'Free Dance Party' and then started inviting people over. Eventually, a whole crowd showed up and kept up the flow when we went to get you." Oli smiles.

Happiness overwhelms my heart to the point of crying. I grab Amelia's hand and drag her into the crowd. The song "Feel This Moment" starts up. It couldn't have come at a better time. I shimmy my shoulders back and then forward in a constant movement, guiding Amelia.

I throw my hands in the air, shaking my hips around and around. "Follow me."

My body is moving in ways that I've completely forgotten about. It's been so long since I've felt so happy. Looking over at Amelia, she's smiling—completely carefree. The entire crowd stops to allow the two of us to take the spotlight. My body completely takes control. I move my hips into an unending spiral down to the floor and then back up. Sweat drips down my face, but I don't even mind.

Oli throws me a water bottle. *What a lifesaver!* There's no time for a long sip. Through the corner of my eye, I see Amelia start to slow down. When it comes to dancing, the flow must continue. That's how confidence builds. The fire cannot go out. When individuals begin to notice others looking at them, the cycle can be destroyed.

Without thinking, I bounce in front of her, waving my arms in the air and jumping, moving my hips from side to side. Amelia's movements tell me that she has gotten lost in the moment, ignoring the cheers of the crowd. Her gaze is towards the love of her life, Oli. They both sparkle at each other. It seems that he is marveling at the moment too much to consider joining. This is what dance can do. The movement is contagious and mind-blowing.

It feels exhilarating to do this as a group again. I miss this so much. Back when my parents had me in after-school dance classes, I felt that I belonged. The other boys and girls were just as shy and embarrassed as I was. We all followed what the teacher said, not understanding how all the pieces would come together. For months, she kept saying to stop being so stiff. Not knowing what that meant, I assumed I needed to do the moves more precisely. It wasn't until after I had to be unenrolled that I understood what she meant. Dancing is similar to the waves—how they flow where the wind takes them without pausing, thinking about it, or correcting.

The street dancing goes on for another hour, when people start to trickle about their day. It's hard to believe that people randomly participate when there is any kind of music playing. If only there were more fun moments like this back in Miami. The police would most likely not allow it as loud music is frowned upon in certain places. In the city, apartment buildings are scattered all around, and making too much noise can get you thrown in jail.

The three of us are extremely exhausted. We press on to the next surprise, although they kind of gave me a hint of what it would be. There is much to see in Sydney. Downtown alone has thousands of hidden gems that could only be found by walking around or by knowing someone who actually lives here.

I break the ice by inquiring, "So, what's the surprise?"

"You mentioned that you are here on a mission to get to know bugs better, right?" Oli asks with a huge smile on his face.

"Yes. Actually, I have a confession."

"What is it, Eve?" Amelia looks concerned.

I rub my hands, nervous to let this out now. "You see, I lied to you both. I don't think bugs are cool—not even in the slightest. The main reason I'm here is to find ways to get over hating them so much. I'm absolutely terrified of the sight of them."

"Well, that explains a lot." Oli chuckles.

"What do you mean?"

"At the bug museum, your face looked scared the whole time we were there. I can tell you were trying to hide it. That's why I didn't want to be a prude."

"Oh!" I laugh. "I was trying so hard because you looked like you were enjoying the moment so much. I also didn't want to be a killjoy."

"In that case, let's do this. I currently have an assignment to study the insects that reside in the city. You can help me by photographing every single bug you see. Here's my camera. It's a little heavy; be super careful with it."

"Oh, I don't know. What if I get scared and drop your camera? I don't have the money to replace it."

"Don't worry! My camera is insured." Oli continues, "Get some good close-up shots. I'll show you how."

"While you two are doing that, I'm going to go find a restroom," Amelia states in clear discomfort.

I think about going with her that way she isn't by herself, but it's a perfect opportunity to tell him. Oli begins showing me the basic camera features, including the zoom, shutter, focus, and color-changing options. Fear grips my heart at the thought of zooming into a bug.

"Hey, Oli?" I gulp.

"Yeah?"

"I have another confession to make." My palms burn with sweat. Here it goes.

"What is it?"

"I er… had a huge crush on you before I knew about Amelia. I've felt so guilty about it these past few days that the three of us have spent together." I blush, trying to hide my face away.

"Oh… I'm so sorry if I misled you." Oli gives me a very sad look.

"No, no, no. Trust me. You did nothing wrong. I just assumed you were single without even properly asking. I should have." I continue, "But I am so happy that you have Amelia. She truly is one of a kind."

"Yeah." Oli rubs his head, blushing all cute. "I am such a lucky man."

Amelia comes back looking refreshed and even more beautiful than before. I can tell she fixed her makeup and put some perfume on. The air is illuminated with the scent of flowers. Something that I would never in a million years think to do. I'm so inexperienced with impressing others.

"Hey guys, sorry for taking forever. I was super sweaty and stinky," Amelia mentions bluntly as if she knows we would never judge her.

"That's alright! You look stunning by the way," I respond awkwardly. It's not every day that I compliment someone else.

"Oh, thanks." Amelia blushes.

We start walking around the town looking for nature that exists within the Sydney downtown. The skyscrapers are huge, much bigger than in Miami. Architecture is extremely important here as it reflects the country's cultural values. A light rail network goes through the heart of downtown. Sculptures bring the setting to life, making it impossible to forget. Although there aren't many places to stop to take pictures of bugs.

Like any city, nature is very limited to small trees, gardens, and corner parks. Oli points out our first encounter, who is flying close to a flower on a small tree. Without spooking me, he grabs onto my arm, pulling me forward but not too close. I zoom in with the professional camera, trying my best not to gag at the sight of those nasty little orange legs. Its head and body are black with little yellow stripes and two large black pinchers near the mouth. My first instinct is to run, but now I have a duty to Amelia and Oli. Now isn't the time to let my fear take over. I have to be strong for their sake.

My finger holds the shutter button slightly to be able to focus on a perfect shot. *Ready. Go.* A small family walks by the tree, allowing the paper wasp to dart away before my eyes can even notice it's gone. I rush to check the photos to make sure that I caught it in time. *Ugh.* It's way too blurry to be used. My hands must have been shaking the entire time.

"No worries, mate! There will be plenty of opportunities ahead," Oli reassures me.

Amelia pats me on the shoulder. She knows I feel horrible about it. "Give yourself some credit, girl. This is a huge step for you."

Their motivation is exactly what I need on this trip. If only they could come with me to the next two destinations. Suddenly, the area goes from having barely any visible trees to many small trees perfectly placed. Little bunches of hot pink flowers flourish from the tops. I look everywhere only to find out that my eyes do not naturally look for bugs the way that Oli's eyes do. To our right, there's a massive red entrance with Hanzi characters written at the top. Bonsai are placed perfectly to tell visitors what the theme is going to be.

We walk into the magical Chinese Garden of Friendship, immediately welcomed by a koi pond displaying fish of all colors—vibrant orange, bright pink, moon white, and even a calico-colored one. Even though the water looks green and muddy, the fish look extremely healthy.

I send a smirk to Amelia. "Are we taking off our shoes again?"

"Ah, no, not here," Amelia responds, giggling.

Immediately behind us, a little kid shrieks. A tiny brown cricket sits on his shoe nonchalantly as if it is used to seeing humans around. *This is it.* My second chance to shine. I grab the large camera swiftly, zooming in on the shoe as much as possible. I hold focus using the shutter button and press the click. The moment goes by so fast that I barely have time to feel disgusted. I verify the photo to see that I've done it. *Yes. Finally!*

"Whoa! You found a jackpot!" Oli exclaims.

Amelia takes a peek over my shoulder and puts her hand over her mouth. "No freaking way! You captured a rare mole cricket."

I look closer at the photo. *She's right.* Something is

completely off about this little thing. The bizarre features make me look three times to be sure I'm eyeballing this correctly. The hands... they are shovel-like with mighty dark claws. Even the little rounded head and mouth resemble a mole. *Gross, but at the same time, so cool.* The back end definitely looks like a cricket with wings. No wonder the kid is terrified. It looks like a platypus had a baby with a cricket. An alien-like creature that can only be found in Australia.

The couple's excitement is contagious. I cannot believe how exciting it is to find something so exotic that I've never seen before. Still, my hands tremble from moving quickly enough to get a good shot. I pray that Oli gets a good grade even with my amateur photos. Proud of my efforts, I stare into the koi pond with a huge smile.

On a rock, I spot a water dragon soaking up the sun and looking majestic. Reptiles are easier for me to spot. Especially since they roam around everywhere in Miami. Every park has tons of diversity, from iguanas to curly-tailed lizards. I admire them a bit more since they don't actually bother anyone.

"Shall we?" Amelia recommends. There is much to see throughout the rest of the downtown.

Leaving the park feels like we are escaping from a different dimension. It's amazing the different beauties this city holds. When I first did my initial research on Sydney, I found out that it was originally a settlement for convicts. Now, it's a hotspot for the most iconic landmarks and technological advancements. *Amazing.*

"Look! Over there!" Amelia points. "There's a web in the tree. Let's go check it out. I bet she's hiding."

Fear grips my heart since my last experience with a spider wasn't too great. The web is empty, completely desolate. *Maybe she went for a hunt?* Wait a minute, why am I calling it a she? It's not even here, so now we can move on.

"Wait, I see her. There underneath the leaf," Oli says.

I get a glimpse of a big, light pinkish-white spider with a large bottom. I tremble. Goosebumps cover the entirety of my arm. It takes me a minute to pull out the camera. Luckily, Oli and Amelia both know my situation and don't try to pressure me to hurry. I swiftly take multiple shots when the spider starts to glide downward on a thread. She hides herself deep within the leaves for protection.

The three of us take a peek at the last photo that was taken. *Wow.* She looks seriously stunning—like a ninja hopping through leaves. I hand back the camera to Oli, thanking him for the experience. Not going to lie, it was fun, but I'll probably never do that again.

CHAPTER 16

I wake up with the realization that, unfortunately, today is the final day in Sydney. I've been to a few places, but not all the ones I had planned for. That's just life; things never go as planned. The Sydney Harbor Bridge is the final destination. I cannot leave here without seeing it. I head out as early as possible, although I'm exhausted. My feet hurt, and I'd rather be in bed sleeping some more. I'm not much of a morning person, especially when I have to be somewhere. I prefer to take my time in the morning getting ready while sipping on something warm to settle my raging stomach. I step outside only to notice that the sky is ultra dark, with clouds moving in fast and the winds blowing harshly. *Of course, there is a storm heading this way on the last day.*

I spoke way too soon. The rain gushes down from the sky, pounding on the hotel roof. How will I go out now? In the distance, trees bend towards the wind, proving the strength of the storm. Even the waves can be heard from over here. The bellhop stands outside, utilizing the shade of the overhang, waiting for guests to come. He notices the terrified look on my face and walks towards me.

"Don't worry, it's always like this! You'll be all right to head into town and still look around. Just keep this umbrella with you."

He's kind enough to provide an umbrella from the hotel lobby. I love the way he encourages my adventure, even though it's looking sad outside. The wind howls worse than a werewolf during a full moon. I debate whether it would be smarter to simply turn around and call it a day. Embarrassed to turn around at the bellhop's advice, I decide to continue.

"Thank you, good sir, for the tip!" I scream back loudly. The wind chops my voice into pieces.

With hesitation, I walk in the direction of the bridge. Rainwater fills up my shoe. *Gross.* It's freezing cold. I know this will bite me in the butt later when I take off my sock. My feet are going to be all crumbly from soaking in dirty water for too long. I contemplate again turning around, but I cannot leave without seeing the bridge.

Out of nowhere, the rain completely stops, and so does the wind. The calm reminds me of being in the eye of a hurricane. Pure chaos all around you, then suddenly, a complete stop. Peace and prosperity start to give some type of hope until the storm moves, bringing you to the absolute worst part of the hurricane: the eyewall. It's where high winds, heavy rain, and the most danger exist. Scary stuff indeed.

Other people walk calmly, closing their umbrellas, acting completely unaffected by what just happened. It's very similar to the random rainstorms in Florida. They just come in the middle of sunshine and then go away two seconds later. Residents are so used to the unpredictable behaviors that umbrellas are no longer needed unless the weather says there is going to be a storm coming. South Florida is well-equipped for strong storms. Shutters are advised to be put up right away, along with getting a decent number of supplies. Schools and workplaces are closed depending on the projected category of the storm.

Even the roads are built to withstand potholes, mud, and flooding conditions.

The bridge features a designated pathway for pedestrians to walk alongside the bumbling vehicles eager to reach their destinations. The relentless honking of horns urging frustrated drivers to accelerate is degrading. Fortunately, I'm not behind the wheel; the responsibility would send my nerves into a frenzy. Skyscrapers paint my view as I watch in awe. Each towering structure tells a story of ambition and progress. I wish this moment could stretch on forever. Beneath the bridge, the water shimmers in a vibrant hue that mirrors the playful color of dolphins. As I stand here looking out at the city and the ocean, the iconic Sydney Opera House graces my senses with music floating towards me.

The perfect viewing spot, displaying a metal tablet with history written all over it, calls my name. Shockingly, there are no crowds today, probably because of the mini-storm that passed earlier. Apparently, the bridge took nine years to build in 1923. It's the largest steel arch bridge on the planet and is the finest natural harbor. It feels good to be walking in an area that has so much history. Fireworks are thrown here during the New Year's Eve celebration.

Up ahead, a group of protesters shouts random things with huge, colorful signs. It's clogging the exit. What are they even saying? My mind wanders at the sight of it. Never in my life have I been part of a rally. Mostly, women are part of the group, with few men supporting their spouses. There seems to be no way out but to move forward. I decide to check out what all the ruckus is about. The protesters' signs have different opinions about love and promoting no more war.

"Power to the people!" some lady screams in my ear.

"God loves EVERYONE!" a man yells.

"Kindness to all!" a little girl shouts in the cutest baby voice I've ever heard.

People seem to be having a blast waving their signs and yelling out their opinions. It's a form of release. Creating change in the world is always a very touchy subject. There are multiple types of opinionated people. First, there's the outspoken, strong-willed individual who is expected to speak their mind and stand up for the things they believe in. Next, the naturally outgoing and super friendly person who speaks their mind even if no one agrees. There's also the person who speaks their mind using facts that offend everyone when the speaker did not intend that to happen. The problem solver finds like-minded people to support the cause. Then there's me, the introverted person who stays private about her opinions. But not today.

"We are called to love one another!" I shout.

"Forgiveness to those who have hurt us!" a man behind me yells.

"Justice to the people!" I scream.

I yell what I feel until I spot Amelia by herself with a sign that says, "BEING DIFFERENT IS GOOD!" I adore her for that. Little blobs of green and blue paint take up the majority of the white space. I wonder if Oli's also here. That creative sign deserves a compliment.

"Hey! Amelia!" I yell and grab her arm, clearly scaring the crap out of her.

"Hey, Eve. What are you doing here?" Her eyes widen in astonishment as she puts her hand over her mouth.

"Why? Is there a reason I shouldn't be here?"

"Well, it's not legal to protest in Australia. Not like in America, there isn't as much freedom of speech."

The wailing of sirens comes closer and closer, the sound tainting my ability to think. Two stern-faced policemen emerge from their vehicle as they scan the scene. One of the officers reaches into his back pocket, retrieving a long, baton-looking stick. *Oh no, he means business.* It's clear that he's not here for a friendly chat. Panic rises within me, frightened by the thought of getting thrown in jail before my flight tomorrow. If I miss the flight, my parents will be furious at me. I can already see the disappointed looks on their faces.

"Uh oh, we should probably leave now. Come quick, follow me." Amelia shows me a shortcut out before a gang of policemen blocks all sides, not allowing anyone through. "Looks like they will start to arrest people here in a little bit," Amelia warns.

We run towards the end of the crowd and slip away unnoticed, pretending to be innocent bystanders. Amelia's sign disappears into the crowd. Who knew protesting about serious things would be that much fun? Maybe there will be a time in the future for another venture here. I personally have grown an infatuation with the palm trees and plant life. The way of life is completely different from what I'm used to. I pout at the fact that it's my last day. Why does time fly by when you're having a good time?

In the distance, I see a cruise embarking. The thought of getting on one reminds me of the disaster with the Titanic. Large bodies of water actually terrify me because of the fact that I don't know how to swim properly. No one ever taught me growing up. My parents are also avid non-swimmers. I'm sure if the situation calls for it, I'd be able to doggy paddle myself out of harm's way. There's no guarantee, though.

We definitely should have been in jail right now for joining those protesters. I let out a sigh of relief, realizing the beautiful sound flowing in the wind is significantly closer. It's the beloved Sydney Opera House. There's a huge difference between seeing it from far away and seeing it up close. The architecture looks like a master in the craft made it. Its sails look like those of a ship.

"You need to see this place at night. The sails change colors and have beautiful lights," Amelia brags. She has every right to. I've never seen anything like it before.

"I would love to check out the opera house, but last time I looked for tickets, they started at around 200 dollars per person," I mention.

"Actually, if you go after a show has started, they usually give you a discounted rate to make up for the tickets that didn't sell," Amelia says, providing me with hope.

The ticket master, radiating with warmth and friendliness, greets us with a bright smile, telling us to hurry before the show starts. She informed us that there's a delightful family-oriented show at a fantastic, discounted rate. My eyes light up. Now that's the deal I was looking for! What a kind woman.

The seat numbers displayed on the tickets happen to be all the way in the back and not next to each other. I realize that I ended up paying for both of us. Money is not unlimited here, but I couldn't let us miss this one-in-a-lifetime moment. Some things are worth paying for just for the experience. Back in Florida, I paid a ton of money just to ride a Ferris wheel at a random carnival that comes by once a year. Normally, those things should be a couple of dollars per ride, but just for the experience, I spent the money.

Although we are slightly late, it seems like we didn't miss too much. A baby green turtle hatches from the sand and feels abandoned by its mom. The baby is trying to make its way back to its family without being eaten by monstrous seagulls. It reminds me of when I left home after graduation. Not knowing what to do or where to start, the feeling of abandonment overwhelmed me. Although not for long. My parents wanted me to return home almost immediately.

I look around to see that many people join me in tears, including Amelia. What a beautiful story. When I was in grade school, Lucas teased me so much about crying that I made a promise not to let anyone see me cry like that ever again. He would say, "You look so ugly when you cry." I did not want to look ugly in front of my peers. Schools are very particular about the classes they put their students in. Each person is hand-picked to be in a certain class based on their skill levels.

My dad did not want me to quit. He taught me the lesson that I needed to be brave and strong to get through life. I'm sure one day it will come in handy. My mom, on the other hand, has always been the "kill 'em with kindness" type. That's probably where I got my compassion from. Although, now that I'm older, it seems to bite me in the butt every time. I continue getting walked all over by bad human beings in an effort to show them a better way.

CHAPTER 17

*S*adness overwhelms me as I board the plane. I hope to see Oli and Amelia in the future at their wedding. This time, I will not object as I did in my dream. Those two were made for each other. It gives me hope that there can be someone out there waiting for me. I pop in my headphones and my eyes doze off.

Where am I? The sign says, "South Beach," along with a few rules urging people not to litter and clean up after their dogs. I am alone, sitting on the sand. The moon shines so bright that its craters are easily visible. It looks like a block of cheese. The unpredictability of whether the waves can drag me into the deep abyss blesses me with goosebumps in the warm summer air. Sharks rule the ocean, being the number one predator to humans. Shark attacks don't happen too often, but when they do, it can be traumatizing. Usually, they tend to happen more in the northern part of Florida, towards Jacksonville or Tallahassee. A seagull comes by, trying to take the food in my cooler.

"Stop it!" I say, trying to save whatever food is in there. Seagulls are little thieves. They lurk on the beach for anything they can scavenge. Those birds are awful at sharing. It reminds me of the movie *Finding Nemo*: mine, mine, mine, mine.

"When are you going to stop moping around and talk to Lucas?" the bird says to me rudely.

For some reason, it doesn't seem like it's a weird thing that this bird is talking to me, as if all animals speak every day. I respond, "Mind your own business. I'm not ready to face that creep."

"The more you wait, the more regret will come." The bird heeds his warning and goes back into the air with its friends. I let out a sigh of relief. There's no one in this world who can force me to talk to Lucas. I cross my arms, blowing air out of my nostrils. *Hmph.*

A turtle walks up next to me, a little baby with the sweetest young voice.

"He's right, you know. You must forgive him," the turtle says.

"But if I forgive him, what if he continues to hurt me?" I ask the turtle. "You don't know the damage he has caused in my life. I'm miserable."

"Just tell him the truth, clarify all these things you've just told me. Only then will you understand all the reasons why." The turtle flaps his arms and legs one step at a time towards the ocean when the rude seagull from earlier swoops down, picking up the turtle with its beak.

"No! Wise little turtle!" I scream.

I WAKE up to the flight attendant nudging my shoulder. Not understanding what just happened, she tells me that we are about to land. The flight felt like literally two seconds.

Enjoying the little bit of time I have left while I wait for the connecting flight, I check out the different stores that exist in the airport. I stopped in Europe, the highest-priced continent in the world. It's super unaffordable even for someone in the middle class. A hoodie alone is deemed to be worth seventy dollars, even though it looks cheaply made. The thin, rough fabric wouldn't be enough to shield me from the freezing cold air on the plane. Nope, I'm not paying for this. I'll ask the stewardess for a blanket.

At least a decent selection of meals is readily available in the food court. Although McDonald's is still the most affordable fast food here. It never gets old, as the food chain brings back such good memories. My dad would occasionally surprise my mom and me with goodies randomly. Miami has a variety of restaurants that offer baked goods. Some days, after a hard day at work, he would stop by McDonald's, bringing me an apple pie or a freshly baked cookie. I miss my parents even though it's only been a week since I left.

Instantly, it hits me. No one is here to protect me. Fear pours in as it always does when I remember my childhood loneliness. My chest feels tight and achy. How will I get through this four-hour layover all alone?

I say a prayer to calm myself down. "Lord God, help me do this. Don't let me be alone, not like when I was a kid. Help me be strong. Keep me safe in the next two countries. I really need you right now. In the mighty name of Jesus, amen."

My terminal, of course, had to be on the other side of the airport, where there are no restaurants anywhere nearby. *Great, I'm now hungry and depressed.* The empty seating area allows me to get some peace and quiet. Goosebumps run over my arms as the A.C. kicks on directly in this area. *WHY?!* I am not about to go back to the other side of that airport to buy that terrible sweater; instead, I peek into my bag to see if maybe I left extra clothes in there. Something fuzzy catches my attention, along with a note, clearly from Mom.

It says, "Sweetheart, you'll need this blanket during your

travels. Please don't be embarrassed. I love you! P.S. Check Instagram. –Mom."

She is literally a lifesaver! However, did she really have to pick this blanket? A Powerpuff Girls logo is printed in pink from when I was a little kid, obsessed with the program. *Yep, definitely embarrassing.* She's always had a good intuition when it comes to knowing what needs to be packed before traveling. My phone buzzes after it gets connected to the airport Wi-Fi. The message is from my mom asking me to check Instagram as soon as I can for a surprise. Hmm, what is she up to?

As much as I'd rather sit here and pout the rest of the time, I click on Instagram, not expecting to see much since I only have thirty-one followers. But then, tears and smiles take over. It's a post with my entire family rooting for me. A collaboration of different pictures of family members with glasses of wine and signs that say, "Cheers! You can do this!" What perfect timing! If anyone knows how to cheer me up, it would be my family. I feel extremely homesick and start getting my ugly cry going.

The last time I felt this lonely was when I moved out of my parents' house and into my own apartment. I never felt the feeling of being completely on my own until then. My mom and dad wanted me out of the house right away so that they could travel. Although all they ended up doing was going on a cruise together. Mom told me that she felt bad the whole time that I couldn't go with them.

Maybe I'll find a hot guy in Madagascar who will love me, imperfections and all. But then again, I'm not here to write a love story. The point is to get over the annoying fear of bugs. People have gotten rid of their fears by doing the things they dreaded most. But why does it have to be this hard? My dad and I used to watch a show called Fear Factor while my mom was at work, although we were forbidden from watching it after we got caught staying up late. We loved the idea of doing a bunch of crazy things for the prize of a million dollars. If that's not motivation, I don't know what is. The part that I couldn't understand was when candidates had to be thrown in a box full of roaches for an hour or walk across a rope high up over a body of water. The challenges were oddly chosen, but that made it more fun to watch.

CHAPTER 18

The tour guide I hired waits for me in the lobby of Madagascar Airport. Rudy knows perfect English. He's as welcoming as can be. A very strong, confident personality. He warns me about most of the rules in the area. The dos and don'ts, including a few unspoken no-nos. Disrespect is highly frowned upon. Eating dinner before showering is unacceptable. People stare a lot. Not many foreigners come to this part of the world. The biggest thing people despise is being photographed without permission. The elderly are highly regarded. Eating is conducted solely with the right hand.

Rudy leads the way to the check-in, where officials check passports, ask questions, and give the luggage back to their owners. One requirement is to be prescribed malaria pills before exiting the airport. The disease can be fatal and is transmitted mostly through a small blood sucking pest, the mosquito. Repellant must always be put on, along with consistently wearing long-sleeved shirts and pants. Nothing can ruin a trip more than the sicknesses that come from drinking contaminated water, insect bites, or influenza outbreaks. Before leaving, all the research I did for each country mentioned being ready to get some kind of sickness. It's simply a matter of not being used to the environment. There isn't necessarily a way to avoid it other than having someone with you who knows what to eat, places to stay, and safe things to do.

Many people around keep looking at me, saying "Bonjour Vahaza," which Rudy tells me is a nice way of saying hello to a stranger or foreigner. Smiles are given each time a new person passes by me. Everyone is extremely friendly here. But the real adventure begins tomorrow. Jet lag can really harm sleep schedules. Back home, I'm used to waking up around six in the morning to shower, eat a small breakfast, and get mentally prepared for an annoying day with Lucas. Lately, it's been so nice being able to sleep to my heart's desire. No commitment or impossible schedule is holding me back from taking care of myself.

No plans have been made as far as employment for when I return. I'll need to find a new job along with a new apartment with a nicer, more patient landlord. Hmm, I should probably worry about this later. Money seems to be an issue for most people living in the U.S., especially people in my age group. Plans can be scary when nothing ever goes accordingly, or so I hear from many people in their forties on social media. Mom gave me the advice to go with the flow of life without complaints. It helps to be more at peace instead of having super high expectations of everything.

Back at home, most days were spent dreaming of what life could have been if I'd made an effort in high school to work part-time and save up for college after my senior year. The worst thing to do is to live in the past with the what-if questions.

Rudy walks me to the hotel that was booked for me through the travel agency I used to figure out the itinerary for the trip. People who live here know this place like the back of their hand. It's difficult to find proper travel accommodations on the internet since there are not many reviews. Even though we are able to use vehicles, we decide to take a stroll instead to get some fresh air after that extremely long flight. The perk of this specific hotel is that it is very close to the airport.

"Get some rest, Ms. Evelyn. I'll be here first thing in the morning," he reassures me.

"Yay, I'm looking forward to it. Thanks for giving me time to rest. Also, you can call me Eve," I declare, not used to people saying my full name.

"Okay, Ms. Eve, goodnight."

Was that a smirk? Another thing, he stared at my hand often, probably looking for a ring to check for my marriage status without popping the question, or maybe he's a weirdo who has a hand fetish. Exhaustion plays tricks on you. I mustn't over-react to something so minimal.

After checking into the hotel in the lobby, I make a beeline to my room. There isn't any air conditioning, but there are large fans shaped like leaves blowing on blast. The warm air feels great after the long hike to the hotel. I'm probably still nervous from meeting Rudy. He's got his own charm that's impossible not to notice. I never know what to talk about and just hope that people don't mistake my silence as being rude or angry. Giving a bad first impression happened often, but it's how I found the sincerest friends. I set my bags down on the corner wall. The bed sheets are puffy and welcome me to plop on them. Yes indeed, don't mind if I do.

I look at the time; it's 2:00 a.m. I start to research the different excursions I'll be going on. Three are included in the package, along with two surprise destinations. First is a cave tour, where we will be visiting mysterious bugs within the cave, and then a safari adventure awaits me. A hike will be the final destination to locate the unique, intriguing insects of this land.

On top of that, I'd like to ask Rudy to take me to the local beach so that I can experience the difference between a beach that has not been polluted by humans. Natural waters, sand on my toes, and finding seashells are on the bucket list for this trip. I take a deep breath and go with the flow instead of trying to make everything sound perfect. It's good to plan things, but overplanning is a huge problem that leads to disappointment. Anything can go wrong, I mean specifically, the weather. If it's too hot, I may just stay in for a day since my skin is sensitive to the intense rays of the sun. Olive brown skin only gets either tanner or red, which makes the skin peel off.

Rudy awaits me in the lobby of the hotel the next day. I only know because I can hear him flirting with the ladies at the front desk; at least, that's what the giggles sound like. He didn't want to knock on my door and wake me from my slumber, as that is considered rude here. It should be a rule everywhere.

Sleeping has never brought me any joy. In fact, it's been harder throughout the years. It feels good when there's nothing to worry about. But when there are many concerns that are unsolved, falling asleep is nearly impossible. Mom used to put a gentle VapoRub on my forehead to help with the process when I was younger. She has always had a knack for these things. The joy of being a parent is waking up when your children can't sleep and assisting them even when you have to go to work in the morning. I can't even imagine the exhaustion of failing to get a full eight hours of rest. Parents are so admirable. I really mean that.

After getting dressed in cargo pants and a long-sleeved shirt, Rudy guides me to the bus stop that comes every couple of hours. If it is missed, it would take at least another four hours to catch the next one. We hop into the tour guide bus that takes us across the savannah to the first destination. All I see all around is staring eyes like I'm a wild animal being displayed in a cage. A random old man offers me some sort of cookie, which is sweet, but Rudy tells the person, "No, thank you," in his native language. I dodged a bullet there since, in my eyes, it's rude to say no to someone who is offering a gift. Good thing Ruby is here watching over me. Getting trapped into giving someone money is something my heart would fall for in a heartbeat. Seeing people in need all around truly docs hurt. There are homes built very small yet efficiently for one person, although the average family in Madagascar has about four to five people.

The view out of the bus window looks very peaceful. There aren't many tall buildings like in the United States, but every place serves a purpose. There are stands for coconuts, vegetables, meat, etc. Many farms exist in the area, mostly harvesting cotton, tea, dairy, and rice. People live sustainably, but I've heard wages aren't that great because the cost of living is different. The most a typical family would be paid per month is about twenty to thirty dollars. Rudy mentions that as long as the children are fed, adults will sometimes go days, if not weeks, without eating anything to ensure the success of the next generation. Going to school is a luxury.

The savannah looks dry; the air feels toasty like I am in the middle of a desert. Luckily, Madagascar has many beaches to cool off. The grass is tall, but the trees look ancient. Mountains are rocky but still manageable for someone like me, even without much endurance.

"Wow, this is beautiful. Do you live nearby, Rudy?" I'm simply in awe, looking around. It feels almost unreal or like I'm in the middle of a cool dream.

"Yes, I help out my parents every weekend on their small farm," he says. "I'm very familiar with the cave we are going to. I go there often to harvest mushrooms."

"Oh wow! That's amazing. Do you sell them?"

"No, we live off the land and trade with our neighbors."

What a great system to have. Not to be too worried about money all the time, but just relying on what the Lord provides, just like birds. In fact, we should all be living this way. Helping neighbors instead of being super selfish. I know for a fact that farm life would not be good for me. Harming even a fly is impossible. I cannot even think about killing an animal. I wouldn't be able to even if I were starving. Going vegetarian sounds like a great choice right now. Time is irrelevant as the way of life is much slower and more peaceful here.

Finding the cave is quite easy since the land is flat. Having the right shoes this time plays a huge role in the success of walking from the bus stop to the cave. I brought a small fan to hang around my neck. It's the smartest thing ever. I wish I could take credit, but honestly, it wasn't my idea. Mom mentioned that it might be hotter than Florida. It is one of the perks of having Cuban parents. They know what to expect when going to another country.

The mouth of the cave is eerie, like a lion about to devour its prey. There is a huge difference between light and complete pitch-black darkness. It smells like a wet penny that has been sitting inside a water fountain, corroding for millions of years. Rudy specifically tells me not to touch any walls. If the walls are touched and I accidentally put my finger in my eyes or mouth, there could be consequences; although death isn't mentioned, I find myself worried anyway. Then, suddenly, my fear is extinguished. A glowing river provides light to the cave. Apparently, it leads to the ocean, and fish can be caught using this hole.

Rudy grabs a stick while installing a line to it. A substitute for a weight, a rock is placed at the top and tied around the line. He uses a nearby wild mushroom as bait. I can tell he has been doing this for years. Fishing is a local favorite hobby and a way to get a meal on the table without sacrificing one of the farm animals. We both sat there waiting for a fish to appear, but none came. I see Rudy whispering a prayer, and then he casts up his line. Getting caught up in the moment, we move on to walking deeper into the cave with torches in hand.

Bats squeal, flying away for dear life. There is an old myth that a creature called Chupacabra would come out at night hunting for little girls like me. Kids at school, including Lucas, would tease me about being afraid. News reports mentioned farm animals randomly dying from an unknown cause. Although I was a smart kid and never believed a word they said. It was probably just a way to scare people and make some money. It's similar to the ghost tours that are offered in certain towns that have been around for years. It's just a marketing tactic to get a quick buck. But this cave, it's the real deal. The sounds of dripping water all around can really freak a person out. Who knows what kinds of creatures will appear up ahead? I look up to see that there are huge gashes of rock that look like they could crumble down any minute. Cold droplets keep falling onto my head.

"There! I see it!" Rudy yells.

"What, what do you see?" I'm terrified that it could be a Chupacabra or a giant alien bug.

"Look closely, that's where we are headed next."

CHAPTER 19

*I*n the distance, I see a small boat waiting in the sparkling, crystal blue basin. The water looks as if there are magical crystals within it. Caves have never interested me. I'd always heard that bats take up this territory. Bats are associated with vampires, which scares me. Although in school, they do teach that bats have the greater purpose of hunting down mosquitoes.

"Eve, see the markings on the walls?"

"Yes, what are they?"

"In ancient times, our ancestors used to live in these caves. They left a map," he goes on, "for those who are worthy to follow; only time will tell what we will be seeing." I can tell that Rudy is good at building up suspense. It worked.

Wow. I didn't know there was going to be a hidden path on this tour. The travel advisor only mentioned that there's a walk-in path going in and out the same way. Should I trust this guy? Anxiety tells me no, yet the sense of adventure tells me yes. I notice that for the first time, I feel like listening to the latter more.

The markings display some of the first human art ever formed in caveman days. They look peaceful, showing families who were fishing in the beautiful blue water up ahead. An illustration of a campfire cooking the fish on sticks reminds me of making s'mores with delicious bars of chocolate and marshmallows. *Yum.*

The small boat is difficult to climb into. Rudy takes my hand, lifting me up onto it. I can tell that it's been passed down for generations since the paint is very chipped. Pictures are inscribed on the sides, and there is a spot to put our torches. Rudy grabs a paddle and hands one of them to me. Yay, it's time for some upper and lower arm exercises.

It's been a while since I've had time to work out my arm muscles by "swimming" in the ocean. More like doggy paddling my way through those intense waves that wash you away in Miami. Once, Sarah had to save me when my shorts flew off during one of the jumping wave sessions that are hosted every summer. Luckily, she had an extra that wasn't needed for that very reason. If not, I'd have to wear a towel and head home instead of continuing the fun. People lose their clothes at the beach all the time, along with valuables like purses, wallets, phones, headphones, speakers, etc. Normally, when we go, we have other friends come; that way, someone can watch our possessions on the sand, making sure they do not get stolen.

The writings on the walls continue throughout the way, symbols that I've never seen before, seeming like they were either warning about something important or leading to a breakthrough. As we paddle through the glowing river, the boat feels so peaceful. Not bumpy or swaying like being in the ocean. It's more of a smooth ride with excitement about what's to come.

"Do you ride this boat often?" I ask Rudy, simply to make conversation. He's extremely understanding of being in silence.

It makes me happy to know that there is someone else out there who enjoys peace. I could talk up a storm when I'm comfortable enough. Other than that, I have to force words out of my mouth.

"No, only when there's someone brave enough to request a ride on it," he continues. "It isn't normally part of the tour, but my parents told me that when I find someone worthy, I can take them with me."

"Oh. I'm glad that I somehow fit that description. What are the qualifications?"

"Well, being a pretty girl is one of them." He chuckles.

"Aw, thanks. That's sweet, yet kind of creepy. Where are we going?" I wonder if Rudy takes any girl that he thinks is pretty on this boat ride. Maybe I'm not the first.

"You'll see the entire cave this way. There is nothing to worry about. The end of the tour was before the boat ride."

"I see."

Things get slightly awkward. Offended by the thought of Rudy trying to woo me, I don't feel like talking to him much. Luckily, I heard that Rudy is a very trustworthy tour guide, one of the best they've got. I did lots of research, along with reading tons of reviews, just to make sure everything was going to be safe during my time here.

Finally, we reach a stopping point. Mysterious blue lights twinkle and glow all around the cave, casting a mesmerizing shimmer across the rugged stone walls. They wrap around the majestic tree, steady and firm in the center of the cavern, creating an enchanting atmosphere. It reminds me of a festive Christmas light display. As I stand in awe, the lights pulse gently, illuminating the cave with their ethereal glow, trans-forming this hidden place into a breathtaking spectacle. Amazing. Truly phenomenal.

"Wow, this is gorgeous! How is this possible so deep within a cave?"

"They are called glowworms. During this time of the year, they are finding a mate to spend their lives with." Rudy blushes, turning his face towards them.

I beam at the constellations, feeling so happy to have this opportunity to be here right now. I am thankful for my family, who thought of me even before I was born, or else none of this would ever have been possible. My parents are so understanding about my dreams, instead of being like others who force their children to be doctors or do something with a more stable income.

Other than a few more colorful beetles and mushrooms, the glowworms are the biggest highlight of this cave. Rudy seems like he had something to say, but ends up holding it back. I wonder if it has anything to do with the comment from earlier. I'm no romance expert, but he seems to be attracted to me. Why else would he willingly call me pretty? Also, why did he take me to a place where only "special people" are allowed to go? It's all very suspicious.

Back to the scary mouth of the cave, I am surprised that so far, all the bugs in this country don't seem to be the annoying ones back home who chase you when they smell your fear. Other than the occasional malaria-infested mosquitoes, it's not nearly as bad as I assumed it would be.

We ride the bus back to the village, and Rudy takes me to a local restaurant to try a staple food that everyone knows. It consists of rice with collard greens on top and a side of onion gravy. Some cooks like to put deep-fried meat cutlets paired with rice. One bite is all it takes to fall madly in love. All the flavors come together, melting inside my mouth. I ask the chef for the recipe, but she tells me that the only way to get it is to accept a marriage proposal from Rudy. *Say what?*

Thinking about such a huge commitment just to get access to a recipe is ridiculous. It is a joke, of course. A few people in the restaurant come over to ask where I'm from. I explain my purpose of being here, along with my ethnicity and family. People around here don't get to go out much due to the high costs of international travel. Their heart is in the right place since they end up asking tourists about their experiences. One of the locals overhears the conversation and comes over to try to convince me to stay in the town. I'm unsure what the motive is. Rudy also starts to bug me about it.

"Thanks for the offer, but I'm sure that I want to go to the next destination after all of our tours," I tell Rudy, hoping all these questions will stop since they're making me uncomfortable.

"I understand, Eve. Anyway, let me tell you about the culture here," Rudy says.

"Yes, I've been dying to find out where everyone is from." I'm all ears.

"There are twenty tribes in different regions with a mixed culture from Africa, England, France, India, and Indonesia."

"No wonder everyone here is beautiful. You all have sexy genes!"

"Yes, that's right. So, did that change your mind about staying here?"

"No. But nice try."

Getting back to the hotel, Rudy looks sad and very puzzled, but I can't tell why. Maybe because of all the talk about other places I've been to. I'm assuming that he just feels stuck without any way out of here. Getting a passport can be very difficult, not to mention expensive. Generations after generations have molded the culture into what it is today. Most of the country has different religions, but mostly Christianity and Islam are practiced. Some still follow indigenous religions as well. Many cultures have their differences, yet they all stick together for support. It's a beautiful thing to see.

Only five percent of people in Madagascar have access to

Wi-Fi. However, many businesses do have it, like this hotel. It gives me the opportunity to call Sarah. She has been assigned the duty of updating my parents and our other friends on the journey.

"Hey, Eve! How are things in Africa?!" she says with tons of excitement.

"Things have been so great. All the people here love me and keep on begging me to come live here with my tour guide—as in getting married to him," I tell her with instant regret.

"Uh oh, is he a potential love prospect? Tell me everything."

"Well," I continue, "first, I need to make sure about something. I need you to promise me that everything I tell you remains between us."

"Of course! But wait, you know very well that your mom has her ways of snooping things out of me. Once she asks a question, she immediately knows that there is more to the story. I'm so sorry. I'm unsure if I can keep that promise."

"Huh. No wonder she's been quiet. She has a source for finding out information. She's waiting to bombard me with questions once I get home, isn't she?"

"Most likely. Now come on, spill the beans."

"Okay, fine. His name is Rudy. He has gorgeous Asian eyes with a very strong body and works on his parents' farm but also does tours as a part-time gig."

"I see, I see. And does he like you?"

"Ugh, why do you just assume?"

"Because what's there not like?"

"You're the sweetest. Honestly, I'm not a hundred percent sure. He is a little harder to read since he holds back most of his emotions."

"Whoop, I knew it."

"Anyway, I'm not really looking for love right now. Then again, who knows?"

"Follow your heart. You know I'll always support you. Just be careful. I miss you."

"I miss you, too. I'll be back soon."

"You better be! Things are getting boring without you!"

"Okay. Gotta go to bed. Sleep well!"

"You too, Eve. Bye!"

I hang up the phone with tons of motivation to hurry things up. But at the same time, it has to feel like I'm improving myself. So far, the resentment towards Lucas has only somewhat faded. It's the longest amount of time I've been away from him. Now, do I ever want to be in his presence again? Absolutely not. If those memories could be removed, I would do it in a heartbeat. These things take time. Although it does feel like I'm just running away from problems, only to come right back to them.

I say a small prayer asking God to help me forgive those who have hurt me. To heal from all the pain and memories that have held me back for so many years.

"God, please help me forgive the people who have hurt me. I know that they are not the enemy but are being used by the real enemy. Heal me from all the pain and bad memories that have held me back for so many years. In the mighty name of Jesus, amen."

Therapy has always sounded like something I'd be interested in, but what would my family think of me? All the movies about people in strait jackets have destroyed the perception of it being a good thing. At this point, who cares what anyone thinks if it is going to help get me through this? Even the most respectable people have to take good care of their mental health to be able to thrive in this hard life.

In high school, a guidance counselor once spoke to me. She didn't have a lot of good advice about the situation other than "Be more assertive" or "Stand up for yourself more often." That experience of a lazy counselor not wanting to do their job has made me resent adults who work at schools without the proper passion. Nothing was ever truly done about the bullying problem. Teachers turned the other way, along with my own family members. It's the reason why thinking of going to therapy would be so difficult. What if they see my pain as invalid, just like everyone else? Or tell me that I could have made more of an effort to make a change on my own?

CHAPTER 20

a small orange propeller plane awaits us from a distance. I wasted most of the night overthinking my life and what to do about Lucas. Around two in the morning, my eyes finally gave out. Sleeping in has never been a specialty of mine, especially due to the crazy dreams that come haunting me randomly. I hate being late. Unfortunately, Lucas would say something, even if I came in one minute late to work. He acted like a drill sergeant who had an obsession with their job. It's hard to believe he has these romantic feelings for me. Being late for any event gives me a ton of chest pain paired with occasional panic attacks.

"Vazaha, welcome!" The pilot smiles at me intently. He didn't seem to mind waiting there. Food plates sit all over the front of the plane. I hurried and worried for nothing.

"Hey, sir, thanks for waiting. I had trouble, er... sleeping last night," I hesitate to say, not wanting Rudy to start asking questions about what happened. My situation can be embarrassing and hard to talk about to someone who didn't witness it.

"That okay, we go now," the pilot says in broken English. I'm flattered that he tries his best to understand me. It reminds me of when family members fly in from Cuba to visit us; they usually speak some type of English mixed with Spanish and are super confident about it. I wish that the confidence they had rubbed off on me before they went back home to their country. Our family always seems to have the kindest hearted people mixed in with the funniest spirit. They love to party and drink, although that's not necessarily my forte; being around them and seeing how much joy they have, regardless of their situation at home, is comforting. Being near people with accents helps me feel somewhat at home, too.

Rudy helps me onto the back of the plane, buckling my seatbelt tightly. Seriously, what a gentleman. He hops into the front seat right behind the pilot as if he's done this millions of times. I don't sense fear in his eyes. I've only ever been on the usual commercial planes—the kind with an enclosed cabin. The air simply circulates to make sure the cabin stays pressurized. The biggest issue is when someone decides to fart or throw up, and the smell lingers the entire plane ride.

This one, however, is wide open. If the pilot decides to do a barrel roll, we may all meet our demise. Not to mention, my hair is going to hate me afterward. Air naturally dries it out without fail. It'll have to be washed and reconditioned right away, as long as the pilot, Rudy, and I are brought back to safety, that is. The plan is to hover over the safari all the way to the east side of Madagascar, where we will be landing to explore the different animals and forest life. It's supposed to be a very peaceful experience that has had many five-star reviews in the last few months. At least, that's what I thought until this crazy man started up the plane. A loud, terrifying, screeching noise echoes in my ear.

"Yikes! That doesn't sound good. Is this plane safe?" I yell in the direction of the pilot, whose name is still mysteriously unknown. Rudy doesn't bother introducing him. *Oh no.* Is this a scenario where the pilot is Rudy's long-lost uncle, who actually doesn't know how to fly?

"Yes, it need oil change. I do it now," he replies without a care in the world as if nothing dangerous is happening. I can only imagine the terrible situation we would be in if we had taken off without the oil being changed. I say a prayer to reduce my negative thinking. "Lord God, keep me safe on this adventure. There is clearly a safety violation, yet everyone is acting calm and collected except me. There isn't even a crew chief to help guide the takeoff properly. Calm my worried soul. That's in the mighty name of Jesus, amen."

"How did you learn how to pray like that? Your faith shines brightly," Rudy says. I've never been told that before. In fact, I've only been told negative things, never anything good.

"Well, Rudy, in times like this, when you're alone in a random country, you have to believe that there is a savior right here for you."

"Can you teach me?"

"Absolutely. Put your hands together. Now, out loud or silently, pour out your gratefulness, your fears, and requests to God the Father."

Rudy stays in prayer for nearly ten minutes. A tear comes out of his eyes. He is truly in deep prayer. What a magical moment. I never thought that my faith could impact another person completely by accident. I smile, happy that I've done something good for once.

The pilot finishes the oil change and checks his tires along with all the gauges. In my opinion, all these things should have been done before we got here.

He lets the engine warm up for a few minutes. Then we take off without warning. The wind flows through my hair. Butterflies jump willy-nilly in my tummy, just like the first day of school or like getting on a roller coaster that's high up in the air. I regret doing this. I put my hands on my face to protect myself from looking down way too much.

"Eve! You cannot miss this! Open your eyes! Here, please hold onto my hand," Rudy yells loud enough for me to hear over the rumbling of the tiny engine, but fear prevents me from putting both hands forward. Only one decides to move.

"That's it. You're going to be okay!"

"Rudy, I'm scared."

"Soon, you'll be seeing the beautiful animals and many of the bugs you told me about. You are a strong girl. I believe in you."

No one has ever believed in me before. Not even my elementary school teachers, who bragged about me having the best grades in the teacher's lounge. I knew all the gossip because I used to go to the nurse's office often to get away from Lucas and his friends. The school nurse knew it was all a lie that my stomach hurt that much, but she had sympathy anyway. I've always been so thankful for her.

We soar through the skies, seeing the tops of mountains and large trees that only exist in Madagascar. Birds are probably wondering why there's a giant machine in the air. It's adorable how they stick together and find food out of nowhere. They truly are free to do as they please. No pressures socially, no bills, and definitely no restrictions.

The east side of Madagascar presents a striking contrast. The savannah appears much drier in the west, with its golden grasses swaying gently in the warm breeze. Going eastward, the humidity envelops us, transforming the landscape into a lush oasis of vibrant greens. The colors shift from dusty brown to emerald hues. The beach is this way, too.

With Rudy's hand firmly clasped in mine, I get the courage to lean out to the right side. My heart races with excitement. I catch sight of creatures playfully darting through the underbrush. A wide, muddy river sprawls, teeming with murky water. The animals residing there are unrecognizable, but from this high up, they look enormous.

"Rudy, are those hippos?" I ask curiously.

"No, they went extinct many years ago. What you see are cows who ran away from their homes," he yells back over the sound of the engine.

That's shocking. I thought that Madagascar had animals similar to the ones on the mainland, like giraffes, lions, hippos, zebras, etc. Cows leaving their farms is probably for the best; that way, they can live a little longer and not be eaten. Back home, there are farms, but not in the main city of Miami. They are located south, where there is more open land. Some of the locals are able to have chickens with the correct permits.

Elizabeth's parents once had chickens in their backyard. I remember their evil rooster attempted to attack me as I helped her pick up some eggs. He probably thought I was a thief trying to sabotage his future babies. Not long after that incident, Elizabeth told me that her neighbors complained about the crowing, and the police came by to pick them up. That was the last time we ever saw them. It was only recently that I found out that her parents never had the proper permits to handle the chickens in an HOA community who have strict rules against farm animals. It lowers their property value, but in my opinion, farming makes the world a better place. It's more sustainable than buying meat or eggs at the grocery store without knowing where they came from, not to mention the steroids that were injected into the animal.

A small plot of land appears ahead, clearly marked by a black crooked-looking circle. Oh no, we are about to land. I hate this part, even on regular planes. This can be either an easy, flawless landing without throwing up, or it can be an utter disaster with the plane exploding.

The pilot lowers the plane, moving left, right, then straight again due to the wind. The motion itself makes me nauseous. The feeling of a volcano erupting inside me starts to poke out of my throat. Instead of letting it loose, I swallow it whole. *Oh no. I can't hold it.* The next round of barf comes out, but this time in the most unexpected, embarrassing place.

CHAPTER 21

*R*udy looks disgustedly at his soaked T-shirt, which was once white but has now turned into a dark poop-brown color. *Gross.*

"I'm extremely sorry, Rudy, I couldn't hold it in," I plead.

"My plane!" the pilot complains in agony. The throw-up ended up falling all over the seat where I had sat for the past twenty minutes. It was already dirty, literally filthy with trash, way before we got buckled into the seats. Maybe this will get him to clean the poor thing. I pray that I don't get charged extra for the mess I've caused. Tour guides tend to take advantage of these situations to get more money in their pockets. Luckily, Rudy is a good guy.

"Tsy azy izany. Mamelà azy. Nahatsiravina ny fipetrahanao," Rudy yells at the pilot, who backs off immediately. They get into a heated discussion, almost throwing up fists until the pilot walks away into the forest, I'm guessing, to clear his head. I feel so guilty.

"Rudy, what did you say to him?" I ask.

"I told him to forgive you, that it wasn't your fault he had a terrible landing," he says, wrapping his arms around himself with his eyebrows curled.

I caused them trouble. It needs to be fixed. I want to make this better. The pilot is nowhere to be found, sadly. There's no point in going after him. I'm already feeling sick to my stomach to the point that I have to sit down. Rudy hands me a water bottle and helps me sit down under one of the very large trees to cool down.

Motion sickness doesn't happen very often, but when it does, it's hard to bounce back from it. Usually, a headache takes over, prompting me to sit in a dark room doing absolutely nothing for the rest of the day. Mom always puts VapoRub on my head to get the cooling sensation happening while my dad complains about being too soft with minor sicknesses. In his defense, before retiring, the era was completely different. It used to be frowned upon to leave work or school early to handle anything. Older people have told me that I'm being a "baby" about it and should just take painkillers and call it good.

Taking care of myself is a top priority now more than ever. There has never been a moment of regret when it comes to making sure that my health is going the way it should as a young adult. My doctor often scolded me that vitamins are essential, even though women stop growing at fifteen years of age. I'm perfectly happy being a five-foot-one young lady who cannot even reach the top cabinet where pots are stashed in my apartment kitchen.

Rudy removes his filthy, throw-up-infested shirt and throws it into the grass. He obviously doesn't plan on bringing that thing back home. Traditional washer machines from the U.S. cannot be found in these households. It would have to be washed and scrubbed by hand. There's no way to salvage it after a stain like that. However, wild animals might come around because of the strong smell of stomach bile.

"Rudy, we should probably get going before it gets too late to look around the safari."

"I agree, but are you feeling okay enough to walk?" Rudy says, concerned.

Admittingly, my brain feels extremely woozy, as if someone had punched me with all their might. Rudy squats down in front of me, putting his hand on my head. Um, I just realized that Rudy is shirtless! His body is bulky and very muscular. Has he been working out since he was two years old? One day, I'd like to start caring about my body. Mostly for the benefits it brings when it comes to de-stressing. According to my doctor, exercising releases endorphins that can improve any bad mood. I've also heard that it can improve sleep and take away some unwanted dreams. Instead of walking, Rudy picks me up for a piggyback ride to get the ball rolling. Time is ticking.

"Hey Rudy, can I ask you something?" I have to know.

"Of course. What is it?" Rudy retorts.

"Well, who is the pilot exactly?"

"It's very complicated."

"There's plenty of time to explain. Will you?"

"He used to work as a helper on my parents' farm long ago, that is, until I was old enough to take over the position. You see, we could not afford to pay for a helper. He has held a grudge because of it."

"I see. How did he become a pilot?"

"As a way to make it up to him, I put in a good word at the travel guide agency that I work for. He got his pilot's license and was provided with that small plane."

"That was so sweet of you to do, you know that?"

"Yeah, well, I owe him."

"Rudy, you don't owe him anything. Your parents had a valid reason to let him go. Money is hard to come by."

At last, we make it to the entrance of the safari adventure. The huge sign in big letters gives it away. A man driving a jeep-looking green vehicle awaits our presence, with a nice lady in ranger gear holding the door open. Her body is well-built, just like Rudy's. The vehicle seats are not very comfortable. The hard material sticks to my thighs, but at least no seat belts are required for the ride.

Rudy speaks to them in Malagasy while I sit here in awe, looking out the window. Lemurs, lemurs, and more lemurs everywhere around the vehicle. There are all kinds of different colors, such as chocolate and black, and some have multiple colors. There is even an albino lemur who doesn't have any eyebrows. They are all so adorable, fluffy, and extremely friendly.

One of the lemurs takes residence on the windshield, forcing the driver to stop the car, as per park protocol. It has a white head, a brown body, and a familiar black face. When I was a kid, there was a show I used to love to watch that entailed learning about animals. The main character was a lemur that looked just like this one. He was so loved and valued by every person in my age group at the time. Rudy translates for the driver and tells me that people in the country love animals. They are well-fed and treated as equals. The safari is one of the main attractions in the area, other than the beach on the coastline. Before leaving on the trip, Sarah wanted me to get her some seashells from Madagascar. She read a story on social media that displayed a beautiful pink necklace that can be made from specific seashells that are only found in this country.

The number one rule on this safari is not to step one foot out of the door of the vehicle without permission or even think about rolling down the windows.

Up ahead, Rudy points at a creature that can only be found in Madagascar. It's called a fossa and is a meat-loving, chicken-stealing little munchkin. It appears to be up the alley of a rodent mixed with a sea otter. Its skin is luscious brown with cute little bear ears. Getting closer, it has the capability to bite my finger off if I make it upset enough. Next in line turns out to be the famous reptiles of the land. Iguanas roam free to eat as they please. Giant chameleons are strapped to trees with their mates and babies. There are all kinds of colors, especially light blue, red, and green. The guide, who is driving, starts talking to Rudy.

"Hey Eve, see that turtle there?" Rudy asks.

"Yes, what about it?" I respond. Never in my life had I seen a turtle grow that large. Back home, all that can be seen are the tiny ones that exist in small ponds and man-made lakes.

"It is a local delicacy here in Madagascar, though too expensive to buy."

"Oh, that's really sad. Don't these guys take many years to get as large as that one is?"

"Yes, hunters poach them, which is why many of them are housed at this reserve."

Knowing that there is a poaching problem makes me very uncomfortable. I know that in mainland Africa, poachers get animals with beautiful skins to sell to those who request them in other countries to create expensive coats. It should be illegal. I'd like to make an effort to support the sanctuary when I have enough funds to do so.

The end of the tour consists of beautiful birds that are also in danger of being poached to be used for unique cuisines and fashion. We thank the guides and head back towards the little plane. Luckily, the pilot is there already, this time with the engine running and ready to go. I want to ask if he is okay, but instead, I keep it to myself.

Takeoff isn't nearly as scary this time. Rudy's comment from earlier had a huge impact on the way he flew. It's steadier, less bumpy. Sometimes, people need a wake-up call when doing something wrong to promote some kind of change. The landing isn't too shabby, either. It's smooth sailing the whole time, but not a word comes out of the pilot's mouth. He and Rudy will

have to talk things out later. I hope I didn't make their relationship worse.

The three of us head to get a bite to eat at another local café,
except the pilot recommended this one. The food is exquisite.
No one wants to spoil the surprise about what the meat is. Déjà
vu hits me from the experience in Sydney. Rudy eventually
gives in and tells me what it was. It is eel with pork, a specialty
dish only found in Madagascar. After dinner, we have a few
drinks called kava. At first, I was very skeptical because it
looked like muddy water. After some consideration, I decided to
give it a shot. It tastes earthy and spicy at the same time. A weird
mix to have. The pilot and Rudy appear to start acting normal
again until a few thugs come rushing through the door.

CHAPTER 22

*T*he room is silent until a loud bang turns everything into a slow-mo. The entire table, along with my food, flings into the air, impossible to save. I planned on bringing it back to my room to eat in the middle of the night. Well, that's not happening. Not knowing how to react, I stand there, shocked. Rudy looks at them intently with an angry stare.

"You! Where my money you stole?" The strange man shouts at Rudy with no remorse. The other fellow with him grabs the broken glass cup from the ground that we sipped kava from and threatens us, pointing the sharp end close to Rudy's neck. Desperate for assistance, I look over to the pilot, noticing a large smirk. He knew this would happen here, didn't he?

"No, no, sir, I do not know what you speak of," Rudy defends his case, throwing up his hands while clutching his fists tightly. Adrenaline is pumping.

"Don't play dumb, boy. I know it was you."

It is apparent that the second thug does not speak English, but something isn't making sense. Why did the thug not speak in Malagasy? He grabs Rudy with the broken glass in hand, threatening without words to stick it into his eyes.

"No!" I scream.

The second thug stares me down, dropping Rudy to the ground. As he walks slowly toward me, I start to think that this is the end, for real this time. *Crap, what should I do?* Running for my life is out of the question. I don't have nearly enough endurance to outrun them, and I'm cornered. My inner animal kicks in. I grab the broken glass bowl in front of me, tossing it as hard as I can at his monstrous face. He screams, huffing and puffing with all his might. In full power and bloodlust, he lifts his arm, ready to thrust the glass into my flesh.

"Wait!" The pilot yells, gasping for air, blocking me from the hit. "Please, you both have gone too far! This is not what I wanted."

"What do you mean? You pay us to kill, am I wrong?" thug number one says, puzzled and extremely confused.

The pilot trembles, ashamed of himself. Customers eating inside the restaurant use this opportunity to flee. I pray someone will call the authorities. They do not. How can I have such high expectations when I sit here motionless, mortified?

Instantly, Rudy flings up, extending his whole arm for a powerful blow right in the kisser. The first thug flies into the back wall, shattering a whole rack of crockery. The second thug, finally getting it, pulls a fast one towards the exit. I have to do something, and fast. He cannot get away. I pick up another broken glass bowl, catapulting it at his knee joint, forcing him to fall over.

"Eve, let's go now!" Rudy screams, pulling me out the door.

"You don't have to tell me twice. Let's get the heck out of here," I agree.

Running towards the entrance, the pilot blocks the way with his big body. Suddenly, the authorities burst through the door, tackling him to the ground. The restaurant owner isn't about to let a couple of thugs destroy her restaurant. I hope she presses

VICTORIA LORIA

charges. Rudy and I book it as fast as we possibly can with limited amounts of energy. *Great, more trauma under my belt.*

On the way out, the police handcuff all three men, who let it happen willingly. Retaliating would only mean more trouble when given a trial. At this point, there is no turning back on what they have done. I don't understand the motive of this stunt. The things that people would do to take revenge are mind-boggling.

"You okay, Rudy?" I ask, genuinely concerned.

"Yes. But I am worried about you." Rudy sobs.

"I'm okay, I promise. Scared a little, not going to lie, but you were so brave."

"Yes. From a young age, we are taught how to defend our family if something like this were to occur," he goes on, "but you did nothing to deserve this."

"Hey, it's not your fault. I knew from the start that your friend, the pilot, had something to do with it."

"He is not a friend. That will be the last time I see him."

"Good thinking."

Rudy walks me to the hotel, looking around constantly to make sure there are no more threats. Who knows if that dastardly pilot hired anyone else to take us out? To think people here deal with those kinds of things often. It is completely unfair and unjust. The pilot literally paid for us to get mugged over a simple comment to fly the plane better. The huge lesson to learn from this is not to hold grudges and fix issues right away.

Lucas has been evil to me for so many years. It's only natural to abhor him. The way he'd talk about me to others as if it were better that I'd never been born. Not being able to communicate or even defend myself became a huge problem early on. Sometimes, I wanted to say, "Can you please just leave me alone? I hate you. I've never done anything to you," but I never worked up the courage to do so. Hurting someone with words has never been the answer. I could have told him exactly how I felt, but I had compassion and fear that it would make him suicidal. The problems with his family and foster families were too great to handle, I think.

When my parents argued about something when I was little, it didn't hurt as much since I knew they would make up the same night. They paved the way in teaching me how to handle conflict the right way. Even my grandma gave me advice to be more understanding of the people who are in need. She never wanted me to succumb to the level of any bully. I ended up finding the best friends I could ever ask for. We weren't necessarily the "popular crowd", but the way we trusted each other through thick and thin made all the difference.

People would say they were weird for hanging out with me. Eventually, it got old. Sarah did her best to protect me at all costs, along with Elizabeth. Sometimes, I wish that home-schooling could have been an option for me. Maybe then I could have grown up into the beautiful, confident woman that God created me to be. Many people have different opinions on this. Being social plays a huge role in attending public school. Those skills are supposed to help children later in life when finding a career. Yet, so far, none of those skills have helped me in any way. In fact, only trauma and lack of confidence have come from it. I promise myself that when I have children in the future, I'll listen to them. Be there for them when they are struggling instead of allowing things to happen willingly to produce "growth". My future children will be loved and nurtured every day of their lives. Not that my parents didn't do a good job—they did the best that they could. I only wish my voice were heard more.

Lucas should have been heard more, too. His father left him and his mom for a random young woman. His mother, who went insane with drugs and violence, attempted to cope with her pain. I wonder if he is actually suffering deep down inside.

Trapped inside his own head and ways of thinking that he learned from a broken household.

I imagine his real self, a loving kid who was never held, screaming inside his heart the things that he wanted to say, but instead, evil words and actions came out. There have been times when I felt the opposite way. Feelings of anger are trapped inside. It's only boiling to come out without a way to. Instead of harsh words to defend myself, loving words take their place. A panic attack starts to arise, forcing me to stop thinking and say a prayer, "Lord God, please help Lucas and me. Our own selves obviously trap us, the past, and pent-up emotions. Give us the strength to move on. In the amazing name of Jesus, amen."

CHAPTER 23

$\mathcal{I}$n the morning, fear came over me that going out there might produce another near-death experience. Never did I think something like that would happen. Faith brought me the courage to continue going on the hike today. I don't want to waste this day when my trip is, sadly, soon coming to an end.

Rudy comes by as usual, like clockwork, picking me up from the hotel. Something seems off with him, though. A shadow of sadness lingers in his eyes as if he's still wrestling with the weight of betrayal. His old family friend turned against everything that once mattered to him for the sake of petty revenge. *What a shame.* A bitter reminder that hatred, when left unchecked, can drive even the most unsuspecting people to commit unspeakable acts without a second thought. Despite the years of torment Lucas has put me through, I can't fathom the idea of harming him. I would never.

The hike is only a twenty-minute walk away. We both agree that paying for a ride there doesn't make sense. I attempt to nudge a conversation, but Rudy isn't having it. Moments like these are understandable to have a decent amount of silence.

These things take time to get over. The sun beams on our heads, about to burst into flames at any moment. Dark hair doesn't do well with keeping body temperatures cool. Normally, back home, I have my hair in a ponytail for professionalism and to get that thing out of my mouth. Since I'm basically on vacation, I leave it loose to flow in the wind as it pleases.

"Rudy, is there anything in this world that I could possibly do to help make the situation better?" I beg.

"What do you mean? I feel fine," he says, staring down at his hands. Obviously, that was a lie that some kind of macho man would spit out in front of all the ladies.

"It's okay to feel upset and even a little scared. Let's talk about it, shall we?"

"No. I do not want to talk about it."

"Okay. Just know I will be here when you're ready."

Silence after rejection is never a good sign. If I were in his shoes, I'd be demanding answers so I understand the way he is feeling. The best thing I can do is pipe down to let him grasp his feelings. Sarah is the best at doing that. She knows when I'm having the worst day ever and need time just to sit there to process what happened. Ice cream always helps, along with watching some kind of Korean drama. Sometimes, it's nice to know that not everyone's life is perfect, as social media likes to display. Comparison kills confidence.

Trees larger than any of the ones I've ever seen in my life create a perfect space to hike since they provide shade. It's almost like walking through a wind tunnel with a scorching hot mist of sweat running down my back. Tree branches coat the ground. The roots make it difficult to walk without staring at my feet. Once, when I went hiking with our group of friends after a super long work week, looking at the ground was not much of a concern. That is, until I tripped on a tiny rock that was barely the size of my thumb. From then on, I've had a strong sense of caution even while walking normally.

Gasping for breath, I beg for a break. Rudy seems to be fine. I take a moment to chug more than half of the water left inside the plastic water bottle, sitting on a nearby log that is infested with moss. It feels soft like the grass my mom and I used to call "cockroach grass," named for appropriate reasons. All kinds of bugs would hide in that grass. It made it more difficult to play with the other children in the neighborhood who would lie in the grass, making grass angels out of their body shape. Shortly after, a roach would attach itself to their clothes, only to be found by the parents later on. Those memories give me the chills.

Sometimes, thinking can provoke senses from that period of time. When I think of bugs, it sends shivers down my spine. I get paranoid that there might be something on me since I'm usually never the one to catch it. Grossed out, I look down at my hand, which suddenly feels cold even though it's hot out.

"Ewww! Oh, Gross." I screech.

I jump up from the log, terrified, flinging the creature into the air. It's my normal reflex taking over. *Yuck.* It looks like an underwater alien. Rudy, of course, being the sweet person that he is, picks up the poor thing, shooting me a very angry look.

"Eve, what are you doing? I thought you said you wanted to stop being afraid of these little guys?" Rudy asks.

"Um, that's not a 'little' guy. It's huge and disgusting!" I retort.

"Okay, but try to understand his point of view. You sat on top of his home. The only way to defend it was to get on you."

"I guess you're right, but how are you able to hold that thing like that?"

"I have a large amount of respect for them. These are called hissing roaches. They make a sound when there's a threat nearby."

"Did I make him hiss?"

"Yes. If you come closer slowly, you can hear it."

I walk two steps forward. It is deathly silent, but then there it is: the sound of a hiss. Gazing towards the log, babies are scattered everywhere, running for their lives at the warning of their mom or dad. The aspect of it protecting its young is cute, but the appearance is still pitiful. Its head is dark black with antennas poking out. The legs look hairy and spikey. Mahogany brown takes up the rest of its elongated body.

"You don't need to hold one or even look at one to conquer your fear. What you need to do is start showing appreciation for what they are doing for their environment."

"I never thought about it that way. So, what do these roaches do for nature?"

"Many plants and animals die during different seasons of the year. The roach is a natural at disposing of material that no longer has a soul."

Rudy starts to caress the creature as if it has feelings. It stays put, enjoying the petting motion. The hissing quiets down. A sense of awe strikes me as it's put back onto the log, returning inside its home. For some reason, it never occurred to me that insects have feelings and boundaries just like we humans do. I always thought they were mindless little critters terrorizing people. Maybe trying to be a "bug enthusiast" is taking things a little too far; simply making peace with them would be good enough for me. Knowing that insects are living and breathing, with families and goals in mind, helps me better understand their point of view. I promise that the next time a bug shows up in my apartment, instead of grabbing the broom, I will grab a piece of paper to guide it back outside where it belongs.

As we continue through the rest of the hike, I seize the opportunity to test out my newborn love. Mosquitos chase me for my blood, buzzing menacingly around my ears. Gnats swirl around my head, interested in the juice that flows through my eyes. Do I swat even one? Nope. The season of change is here. I can feel it deep within me.

Going home looms on the horizon. I feel a sense of accomplishment, yet a nagging sense of unfulfillment stirs inside me. I need to talk to Lucas and finally get this burden off my chest. I don't want to spend another day steeped in regret, knowing that I never tried to fix things between us. It may go terribly wrong, or it might blossom into something incredible. Only time will tell. My drive and motivation pulse through me with the energy I need to move forward in my life.

CHAPTER 24

The magical entrance of the castle entangles me in an everlasting scene. Royals once resided in it for many generations. England had their hands written all over the architecture. Rudy mentions that the royal family tombstones are near the back. Many people come to pay their respects to the ones who did an amazing job serving their country. National identity can be felt all around. Up the large, steep steps with no rails, we see the entire savannah looking stunning in the brush. The air wobbles with humidity as the sun descends more every minute.

"Rudy, do you come here often?" I ask.

"No, I do not. It is important to pay my respects, though," he responds politely.

Rudy stands there reminiscing and tells me about when he and his dad would come to visit. His mom would prepare lunch for the long journey. The wind howls, creating a ghost-like feeling. Trees do not block the wind, allowing the castle to be naturally dusted.

"When visiting the castle, one must come with a friend since wild animals raise their young here. It is the safest place, but the animals can become aggressive," Rudy explains.

"Yikes. What happens if a person goes missing?" I fearfully ask.

"The legal system in Madagascar is not fond of looking for bodies that have been mauled by wild animals or have gone missing. It can take years."

Getting lost in this unforgiving wilderness isn't a simple, minor inconvenience. It could mean our demise if a wild, hungry animal comes for us. I silently pray for safety.

"Would you ever consider moving to a different country, Rudy?"

"I would, but my parents need me on the farm," he says sadly.

"I understand completely. It's hard to leave family behind. When they put so much pressure on you to be a certain way or to run the family business, especially."

"Yes. It is my destiny to raise up a successor for our farm."

"Whoa. That is a lot of pressure." I gasp. "What about a trusted friend or family member instead? Break that cycle of forcing your kids to run the business."

"No. You do not understand. Things have been this way for countless generations."

I went out of line, offending Rudy by trying to offer my crazy ideas of change. He lives in a completely different world with more expectations. Life is much harder when there is already a set path on the day of conception. It's not right, nor is it fair.

My parents wanted me to go to Harvard, but they weren't dead set on me doing that and disowning me for not doing what they told me to do. Studying had never been my interest from the start. Getting good grades was mostly done to get my mind off the situation that was happening at school with Lucas. My parents were super proud of me, along with all the teachers and faculty. But it wasn't enough to make my life any different from what it is today.

"Rudy, I'm sorry. I truly didn't mean it that way," I apologize.

"It's okay, Eve. I did not mean to raise my voice," he says, "I just feel... stuck."

"Everyone feels stuck in their own way, in their own situation, and in their own life. There are too many decisions and life choices that affect us."

"Yes. I agree."

Rudy shows me around the back of the castle, where two tombs reside. We pay our respects and then wait at the bus stop. People normally come to the castle when there's an event going on. The town nearby is only a short distance away, allowing us to dodge our extremely awkward conversation. I hate sparking up difficult, controversial topics that make others upset. However, sometimes it is necessary to give someone you care about a wake-up call. Humans get sucked into their routine, sometimes unaware that there's a problem.

Madagascar was once connected to India eighty-three million years ago. There are gorgeous waterfalls along with volcanic craters. The villagers make the most of their income from citrus fruits, delivering them to most of the main markets. Roads can be dangerous, especially during the wet season when the road becomes strictly mud. All homes are made from palm tree fronds and dried leaves. The people in the village are so sweet, constantly wanting to feed us different dishes. An abundance of fertile soil allows for the freshest vegetables and fruit I have ever tasted in my life. All around the village flows a long stream of water and an abundance of livestock. The mountains alone are gorgeous. Rocky, yet tons of life. Unsure how the small village thrives here, they have at least one other.

"Eve, let's go," Rudy says after we devour our meal.

"Where are we going?"

I don't have a clue. The plan was to go to two bonus places of

Rudy's personal choice. No information has been disclosed to keep the surprise alive. My life will be worth living if it involves more adventures. I know I'm going to miss this.

We climb up a smaller mountain to be able to see the gorgeous views. It truly is a magnificent sight. The air is harder to breathe, so I hold my chest, aiding the process. Rudy kindly hands me his jacket, assuming I am cold.

"This place is beautiful, right?" Rudy proposes a conversation.

"Yes. It is. But I have some questions. How do you know this place?" I ask.

"A family member on my mom's side migrated here with the rest of the village when the area got too crowded in their original hometown."

"Why did they pick this specific spot?"

"As you saw, the land is flowing with water and contains good soil from the crater. People made a life here, but there is hardship," he continues. "Going down the mountain causes blowouts of tires and citizens getting stranded in the middle of nowhere."

"That's a huge move, wow." With such dedication to their family, they would pack up and migrate to a place with a completely different language and culture.

"I thought about coming here. Starting a new life for myself. But my parents might hate me for abandoning the way they have paved my future."

"Hmm, what if your family moves here and brings the farm?"

"Too difficult. It would be hard to transport that many animals up the mountain with muddy road conditions."

"Is there anything that could make you change your mind and start making choices for your own life?" I know this topic might upset him, but I have to ask. To try and make him see what I once didn't.

"Well, Eve. If you stay here, I'd be willing to leave everything behind," he says, placing his hand on my cheek and caressing it like a doll.

"Yeah, no. That's not happening. Sorry, Rudy. Don't put this on me. You know what you need to do," I tease, lightly pushing away his hand.

The village chief's wife comes up the mountain to tell us not to leave quite yet. Preparations are ready for a festival. *How sweet.* I adore the kindness in this village. Everyone is willing to share the little that they have.

A group of women gathers together around the main campfire area. There are no radios, only their beautiful voices. We clap our hands together, laughing as one pretty lady grabs Rudy for a dance. Her cheeks flushed, indicating a little crush on Rudy. *Why does this bother me?* It definitely shouldn't, as there's nothing going on between the two of us.

The village elder takes my hand when she sees that I'm all alone. I follow her lead. Dancing here is so different. The movement in the shoulders flows with my entire body. Everyone is so happy. It's heartwarming. I clap my hands, waving them in the air, getting lost in the beats of the drum. We switch off partners, and I finally end up with Rudy, who is now behind me, shaking back and forth. Our faces meet, grabbing each other's hands and swaying them.

We watch the sunset in peace and then return to the hotel, where Rudy gives me a sneak peek of where we will be going the following morning.

"You will need to bring comfortable clothes to bathe in the water," he says, chuckling.

"Hmm, okay. Thanks for the hint. I'll see you tomorrow."

CHAPTER 25

The next morning, my legs feel sore from walking so much over the past couple of days. I've thought a lot about how I could see Rudy being a close friend for many years. I will miss him for sure. I appreciate the way he stands up for what he believes in. Coming back to Madagascar to visit next time will be happening, except I'll bring the whole crew to experience it.

At last, the smell of the beach hits me. Palm trees circle around, providing very nice amounts of shade. I decide that it would be weird to bring my cute pink bikini. Instead, the conservancy is its own virtue. Rudy climbs up a coconut tree wearing sandals, using his bare hands. It looks painful, yet fun.

Rudy shakes the tree while creating monkey sounds to make me laugh. "Ooh, Ooh, aah, aah." *What a dork.*

Coconuts have a large green husk on the outside to protect the actual coconut from spilling its juices. Rudy takes hold of his machete, cracking the life out of the green part to get to the brown fruit in the middle. He makes a precise small hole up top, handing it over for me to drink the water inside. Sweet delight fills my mouth, although it tastes nothing like the fake ones sold in cans at the store. I've never enjoyed sugar-free things this much in my entire life. Rudy waits for me to be done so that he can scoop up the coconut meat. *Yum!*

During the rainy season, locals don't normally go to the beach. The seaweed can be felt in the toes; it's so gross. Rudy doesn't seem to care. He jumps into the water, dragging me with him. We bonded significantly because of the near-death experience with the pilot almost handing us over to those thugs at the café. The pilot had been released from prison since he didn't actually perform any of the violence. Rudy thinks he paid law enforcement off.

"By the way, Rudy, are you planning on telling the travel agency about what happened with the pilot?" I ask, hoping he'll say he will.

"Nah. I won't. If he loses his job, that will be on my conscious forever. I couldn't live with myself." He sighs.

Hmm, why am I not surprised? The pilot deserves to be fired. What if he were to do something like that to another group of tourists? I don't want to tell Rudy that, though. I know he will object to it. There's no point in ruining this nice moment we are having in the water. I step out to start on my tan. I place my towel onto the sand and put Rudy's towel next to mine so that we can talk more and enjoy the nice view of the ocean. It's completely clear, sky-blue looking waters with exceptional parts containing growing seaweed.

The sea reminds me of peace. There's so much more down there that no one has discovered yet. Even marine biologists have a hard time doing research in the deepest abyss due to the pressure and darkness of the water. How many things in life have I longed to find, but couldn't—because they were just out of reach or hidden from view?

"Rudy, I'm going to miss you; I truly am," I say, staring into the sky.

"Yeah, you know you could stay here with me. We can work on the farm together." Rudy laughs.

"You're so sweet, but I really can't stay, though. There are things I need to attend to."

Rudy grabs my hand. "You know the feelings I have for you."

He makes me blush. It sounds tempting.

I grab his hand as he sparkles, thinking I am going to comply with his feelings.

"Rudy, I have to say, you are such a nice, strong, and amazing person. But you and I have completely different goals. We live in two opposite worlds."

"Oh." He pouts with the most disappointed look I've ever seen on the man's face.

"One day, you are going to meet the perfect girl who is going to love you just as much, if not more, than you love her. I promise."

"Hopefully. I don't want to be alone for the rest of my life."

It's funny because I used to think that. It never crossed my mind that anyone would be attracted to me. Lucas made it seem as if I were the ugliest girl on the planet. I will always have my friends and family, but it will be much harder as the years go by. My mom once told me that friendships became harder to maintain after she got married, as life got busier by the day. I cannot imagine living a life without my friends.

CHAPTER 26

*T*he annoying sound of my alarm pumps me up, yet makes me very anxious to get to the airport. The past few weeks have been the best in my entire life. There is so much to learn from people in other countries and cultures. With the exception of the near-death incident, I would like to do this trip again in the future.

With bags fully packed, I say goodbye to the beautiful ladies at the front desk who have been taking care of my stay. I'll never forget when they checked up on me in the middle of the night when I cried my eyes out over the fact that Rudy and I could have died at that café if the pilot hadn't intervened to take control of the situation. They comforted me with good advice, hugs, and water. The biggest piece of advice I can remember that night was when Liliane said, "Challenges can either make or break us. Which one will you choose?"

I cannot keep dwelling on the things that have hurt me. There will be many more to come, and I have to be strong and ready to tackle them.

Rudy awaits me in the lobby as usual. Not seeing his face every day is going to be very strange. I'm going to miss his company so much. I will always appreciate his annoying, flirty jokes.

"Rudy, good morning!" I say with tons of joy.

"Morning." Rudy stares down at his shoe.

"What's the matter?"

"I just... have one more place to take you. Shall we?"

"But I really can't. What if I miss my flight?"

"No, it will not take long, I promise."

Hesitantly, I agree to his proposal, and we head towards the forest near a large body of water. It looks similar to the one we saw on the plane with all the runaway cows drinking water. Finally, we come to a stop and beam at the horizon. Cows who have escaped from their homes to live a normal life drink from the water without a care in the world. Surprisingly, when we get close, they are not afraid of getting captured. Instead of alarming them, we slowly draw closer, even petting the friend-lier cows. Rudy brings out potatoes that his mom plucked that morning. He chops the potatoes into smaller, longer pieces to feed the cows. Their mouth feels ticklish on my hand. After some skepticism, I am pleased that I said yes to joining in.

"You know, I'm really going to miss you, Eve." He gazes towards me with a sad look.

Rudy tried everything in his power to get me to stay. The truth is, there really is nothing anyone could say or do to make me change my mind. The effort alone is heartwarming that someone wants me in their presence that much. Communica-tion outside Madagascar will be difficult since the internet isn't prominent here yet.

"How about let's make you an account on social media? When you miss me, message me when you have the time to stop at a place that has Wi-Fi. Would that work?" I offer.

"It might work, but I do not have any technology to use this 'social media.'"

"Let's create a profile for you, and later, when you make

enough money, you could buy a tablet or smartphone to communicate with me."

Locals do have cellphones, laptops, and email, but it is harder to find a place that has connectivity. I take a snapshot of Rudy, posting it to his promising new profile. I add myself as a friend, hoping to hear from Rudy again soon. On a piece of paper, I write down his account information along with the passcode needed to get in. Avoiding the two-factor sign-in can be difficult since nowadays, it's a requirement to keep accounts safe from hackers.

Rudy gets on the bus with me to the airport, where we say our goodbyes. It's always so sad to make a good friend only never to see them again. I hope to come back for a visit in a couple of years, specifically requesting Rudy to be my tour guide again. Although a plane ride to the safari will be out of the plan next time. I'm not risking a situation like that again. Tears flood from my eyes, now that the journey is officially over. I learned so much in such a short amount of time. Who knows when a trip like this will be affordable for me again?

I settle into my seat on the plane, the rhythmic hum of engines lulling me into a deep sleep for the entire flight back. I'm so proud of myself for being so brave these past few weeks. As I think about Rudy, I can't help but wonder if he will soon find someone to rock his world. He doesn't deserve to be alone —he's such a genuinely nice guy, bursting with talents that could light up any room. His true purpose will soon reveal itself; he just needs that extra push to step outside of his comfort zone and not let his family dictate what he should be doing with his life. The possibilities are endless if only he dares to pursue them.

～

A DAY AND A HALF LATER, I finally make it to Brazil. From the airport window, all you see is the forest and a hint of the Amazon River. It's unreal that there's an airport there. My tour guide, Pablo, a very nice man with his assistant in training, meets me in the waiting area with a big sign that says, "EVE-LYN". I'm very thankful for this since everyone else knew exactly where to go. A bunch of men playing futbol—it's called soccer in the U.S.—kick the ball with such precision into the goal. Pablo's assistant runs to join the game for a few minutes. I don't mind watching since they were all shirtless and very sexy. *Whoa. What am I thinking?*

After a two-hour boat ride, we get into a private charter boat that is small enough for the three of us to move around comfortably. The brown river leads us forward. I look around in awe. Vines hang from one side to the other, almost trapping the boat. The continuous canopy produces enough humidity to make my hair frizz.

"See that tree right there?" Pablo points.

"Yeah, what is it?" I ask.

"It is called Cacao. It is how we make chocolate and export it to other parts of the world. It can be found all over the country."

My tour guide speaks English pretty well. He seems to have been doing this long enough to know what tourists want to hear. Up above, I see a momma sloth glaring at us. According to Pablo, babies stay with their moms for about nine months or until they get pregnant again. The baby stares at me with a bored glare, tired of seeing people constantly passing through their home. The amount of nature and charm of this place makes it hard for anyone to stay away. There's a lot of wildlife to see. Pablo's assistant speaks less English. I attempt to engage, but that causes him to stare at me with a smile. *Uh, should I be creeped out or flattered?*

Pablo tells me, "Stephen thinks you're pretty."

"Oh, okay. Thanks…" I respond.

Stephen hands me a bottle of water, keeping a close eye on me to make sure I don't fall out of the boat. It's nice to be cared for by someone other than family and friends. He's a good guy; I can tell that there isn't any ill intent from the way he keeps his distance. Men back home can be disgusting. They get super close to a woman they like, expecting to get anything out of it. I wish they knew how uncomfortable it makes women feel. Especially when they whistle. It's distasteful.

"See this area to the right?" Pablo points.

"Yes," I respond.

"There are piranhas that can be caught to eat."

Pablo explains that the meat is a local delicacy that has to be cooked a certain way. Only skilled, talented fishermen are able to catch them. Hmm, I wonder what a man-eating fish would taste like. After all, you can't really go to another country and not try the local food.

Pablo yells at Stephen, hitting him on the head to stop peeping at me. Embarrassed, Stephen turns red, looking in the other direction. Now that I think about it, no guy has ever been shy around me. All I can think of is the bug, Lucas, who was cruel twenty-four-seven. But now I can see that there are better people out there who know how to treat a lady like the queen that she is.

We arrive in the middle of the jungle, where Pablo hands me a pair of very long rain boots. These will prevent me from slipping in the mud. As I start to walk through the muck, I immediately understand the severity. With one wrong move, I could slip to my death. The smell of wet dogs hangs heavy in the air. The rain starts and then stops constantly. Rainforest vibes are much cooler when they can be experienced in person, I realize.

Frogs croak loudly, then go silent as we approach them. Parrots fly everywhere. Their wings come in all kinds of beautiful shades of blues, reds, and purples. Pablo points out a giant camouflaging moth. How in the world did he see it? It clearly has zero fear of people. I don't mind moths or butterflies since they are beautiful and harmless.

We make it to a small village, where everyone is waiting to meet me. I get a hug from each person and some pats on the head like I'm a little kid. These people have no electricity, yet they are completely happy living in harmony. Just like any country, there are cats and dogs, as well as livestock such as chickens, goats, cows, and pigs.

Around a campfire, we gather, telling stories, which Pablo translates for me. A scary story about a strange group of people living somewhere in the forest is told by an elder. She says that they eat bush meat and other "odd things". Apparently, it's not safe to be out too late at night.

"What does she mean by 'odd things'?" I ask Pablo hesitantly.

"Well, they eat their own kind," he explains.

No more to be said. I'd prefer never to come in contact with that village. I'm very pleased to find out that it's very far away from here. *How scary.* Why would anyone do such a thing? *Eve, remember, you said you weren't going to judge local delicacies.* Still, it's frightening.

We head towards a cute little house near a hill. Chickens and pigs run around freely. Banana trees grow everywhere. What an abundance of fruit.

"Pablo, you're a farmer?" I ask suspiciously.

"Oh, yes," he says, dropping the subject.

Is he a real tour guide? The reviews were very few, after all, when I looked before coming here. His wife comes out, giving me a huge hug and speaking a dialect I've never heard before. It doesn't sound like Portuguese. She gives a huge kiss to Stephen, and I overhear her saying, "Filho," which sounds a lot like "Hijo," which means son in Spanish. The logic is that Pablo is not a real tour guide and that Stephen is actually his son. Something fishy is going on. His wife and family are so welcoming that it's hard for me to worry about anything other than this moment.

A cooked whole hog is brought out along with rice and vegetables. There are so many dishes that it's hard to determine which one to taste first. The villagers use the water from the river, boil it, and then utilize it for showering and cooking. The smell of BBQ in the air makes my mouth water. I take one bite of the pork lechon, immediately falling in love with the flavor.

In the past, I thought about going vegetarian. I learned about all the health benefits. I did all the necessary research to start that journey and failed miserably after one week of eating no meat. In Cuban culture, meat is everything. All kinds. I mean pork, fish, beef, you name it. There isn't one dish that doesn't contain some type of meat. I get very weak when I'm low on calories, sometimes causing me to faint, and eating has been the one way to keep me stable.

I continue eating to my heart's desire. No one speaks to each other; food is enjoyed more that way. Pablo's wife looks pleased with my love for her cooking. My face gives it all away. I can't help it. Stephen sits next to me to make sure I'm okay the entire time. He doesn't stare, though, for fear of his father scolding him again. After dinner, Stephen shows me the room I'll be staying in. It feels cozy and protected, although I know that Stephen would not let anyone harm me in any way. Pablo's wife heats up some water in a bucket for me to take a shower. With a smaller bucket within the big bucket, I pour water all over myself. It's crazy the things I take advantage of back home. After the shower, I lie in bed when I hear a silent knock at the door. It doesn't startle me since I figure it might be Pablo's wife asking if I need anything. But to my surprise, it's not her.

"Hey Stephen, what's up?" I say, looking away in embarrassment. There's almost a hint of flirting in my tone.

"Would you like to view stars with me?" he asks, flustered.

CHAPTER 27

*P*ablo taught Stephen the little bit of English that he knew. What a good father. As far as I know, the language is not taught as a priority due to the government not wanting residents to flee. Portuguese is spoken in Angola, Brazil, Cape Verde, East Timor, Equatorial Guinea, Guinea-Bissau, Macau, Mozambique, Portugal, and São Tomé and Príncipe, with the exception of a few people still speaking it in other countries.

"Sure, I'll go with you," I say enthusiastically.

Sarah would be very proud of me. Stephen is so excited that he grabs my hand, walking me out of the house and quietly into the night. He puts his index finger over his lips, indicating that we must stay quiet and not wake the other villagers. He guides me to the river's edge, where the sky reveals itself in all its beauty. The area is all set up for this moment with chairs and a small table. Bottles of water wait for me, along with a box of goodies. Hmm, he must have known that I would say yes to his proposal.

Fireflies flutter past my face, but the buzzing can barely be heard. Not like the sound of flies moving their wings at a hundred miles an hour as they zip past your ear. Some of the fireflies hover over the river as if taking a sip of water or maybe even glancing at their own reflection. There are no mirrors in the Amazon, after all. The locals use each other to check that their outfits are appropriate, or at least that's what I read online.

We don't hold much of a conversation, probably because of the language barrier, which is perfectly fine with me. Being silent is my specialty. I'd rather hear the bugs, birds, and random sounds of the forest. Wait a second, did I just say I'd rather hear bugs?! Maybe this trip is changing me.

Rain sprinkles on my cheeks. Stephen has already prepared for this to happen and holds out warm raincoats. In the Amazon, rain can happen at any given moment. The moon has a mixture of colors: bright white and yellow. The craters are very apparent during a full moon. We stare up into the sky in awe at the number of stars sitting up there without a care in the world. I wish my life could be like this every day, somehow unaware of what's going on but completely aware of the moment. Even without electricity, no cellphones or internet, no running water in their homes, and sometimes fear of the water rising during the wet season, a peaceful life is lived here on this tiny, remote island in the middle of the rainforest.

Stephen points out a giant moth that is bothering a much smaller one. *Get away from her!* Oh, wait, they're breeding. This one is way larger than the one we saw earlier. Rainforests hold an extraordinary importance for the planet. It can absorb greenhouse gases from the atmosphere, along with maintaining the Earth's limited supply of fresh water. *How remarkable.*

"Look over there!" I exclaim to Stephen as a shadow of an animal approaches from the tree. "What do you think it is?"

"Margay," Stephen spits out, not seeming to be nervous at all. I wish I had that type of confidence.

The shadow creeps closer and closer, its silent footsteps

barely disturbing the air. Standing before me is the most majestic creature I've ever seen. Her big paws touch the ground with a heavy grace, yet her body relaxes as she stares into Stephen's eyes. The miniature leopard strides confidently toward Stephen, who kneels with a look of happiness and comfort on his face. He extends his hand, fingers curling invitingly, ready for her warmth and trust as she approaches with quiet elegance.

"Spspspspsps, come, Amora," he whispers with so much love.

Her fur appears voluminous, soft, and luscious. She rubs her head along with her whiskers all over Stephen, sticking her invisible pheromones all over, claiming him. He explains that he found her when she was a baby, fed her, and they've been close friends ever since, he tells me. Stephen also shares that his father forbade him from being friends with a wild animal, but to him, she was everything but wild. I don't get too close in fear of her running away. My eyes can't believe that this is even possible.

"Stephen, do these guys prey on humans?" I have to ask.

"No, no. They eat small things, like frogs," he replies, putting my heart at ease.

I was worried that a whole family would come out of the tree, ganging up on us. A sound from behind us starts to creep up. It sounds like the voices of people in the village. Oh no, they must be looking for us. *Did something happen?* We were warned not to be out at night and broke the rules. Now we're in trouble for sure.

"Quick. Hide with me." Stephen takes my hand, and we both dive behind the large tree while Amora flees away into the forest. I let out a sigh of relief. Her being safe is extremely important to me now that I know her past with Stephen.

"Where are they? Are you sure you saw them here?" Pablo puts his hands on his head.

"Yes, I saw them." The villager looks around guiltily.

"Pai?" Stephen jumps out of the bush.

"Oh, thank heavens. Is Eve with you?"

"Yep, I'm right here, Pablo. Don't worry," I say, my face completely red.

"What were you two thinking?!" Pablo's eyebrows move closer together with his lips tightening. "You do not go into the forest at night alone!"

"Yes, sir, it won't happen again." I look in the direction from which Amora jumped. She's nowhere to be found. Thank goodness she's so smart, fleeing at the sight of hostile humans and their torches. If she had been found, Stephen probably would have been in a heap of trouble. Being out past midnight is frowned upon since anything can appear in the Amazon—from wild hungry animals to dangerous individuals. A few people from the village have gone missing without a trace. *How scary.*

Finally in bed, I still don't regret a moment of any of it. However, seeing Pablo mad reminded me of my papa. I miss him so much. When I get back home, I need to be careful what I tell my parents since they may never let me leave on my own again. This experience is mine alone. No one can take it from me. I hope to see Amora, the beautiful little margay, again. I drift off to sleep feeling relaxed for the first time in a while.

A beautiful man stands before me. Large, sexy, tempting muscles in a black tank top holding on to Amora, cuddling her soft face. He is completely mysterious. Dreamy, almost. His dark, wavy hair blows in the wind. His eyes look at me so intently, inviting me to join the cuddle party. I look around, checking if the scene is safe from the villagers. Before I take a step, a smell in the breeze draws my attention. Mmm, yum, fried chicken. *Delicious.*

I wake up to the smell of food being cooked. Camila, Pablo's wife, has such a kind, sincere heart. I mean, I wasn't even awake yet, and she has already begun preparing a feast for her family. I come out of the room, looking for ways in which I can be of use. She gives me a stern glare, indicating that I should be sitting down and relaxing.

After our meal, we say our goodbyes since boarding is in five minutes. Time isn't taken as seriously here. A few minutes late doesn't hurt anyone, not like in the U.S. We all get on the cruise, where we will stay for the remainder of the time in Brazil. I am given a nice, cold glass of water and an abundance of cheese with ham on a platter. I could get used to this.

Something about traveling makes things so magical. Pablo and Stephen stay by my side at all times, almost like guardians. The safety meeting before departure includes lots of information about the wildlife in the area, such as anacondas and pink dolphins. The rooms are large and gorgeous, with big beds. Luckily, we are able to stay on the same deck. From the windows, the river is very visible. After admiring my room, I go to look around the boat.

The lounging area is stunning. It is perfect for sunbathing, reading, and relaxing. Other than that, the boat is quite small but has everything from a daily-serving buffet to a hot tub on the roof. Looking out towards the river, I spot a few locals teaching children how to fish for piranhas. The kids are ecstatic when one of them finally catches one. Even the children act differently here. It's like they are more aware of their surroundings. They kind of have to be with the amount of wild animals out there.

My stomach rumbles. It's time to go on my first excursion. On a smaller, raft-looking boat, we venture to a nearby village, different from Pablo's hometown. Children await our arrival, giving me a million hugs even though they don't know me. How sweet. Pablo tells them to give me some space, and most of them listen, except for one little girl. I see her peeping at my bracelet. It's pink and made by my best friend, Sarah.

I remember the first time we started giving each other gifts. Sarah has always been the most creative person I know. She's devoted to creating things with her two hands. I made a drawing for her, which was awful, but she loved it so much. That's when she surprised me with this cute pink bracelet. Since then, I've worn it for years, whether it matches my outfit or not.

When we finish eating roasted fish with white rice, a dance party breaks out to celebrate our togetherness. Stephen takes my hand to dance. His father sends over a dirty look as if he disapproves. Can I blame him? I'm simply a foreigner who is not going to be here that long. I'm sure he wants his son to stay away from an outsider like me.

Stephen's hand runs up and down my back, respectful enough to stay away from my bum. The music is fast paced with a nice beat to it. This is the most bliss I've ever experienced in my life. My cheeks feel burning hot, and my heart is pumping faster than ever. It's so hard to breathe. The music now changes, forcing us to a slow dance in which Stephen holds me even closer and tighter. For not being able to properly communicate, this is going quite well. Maybe it's not such a problem after all. In fact, it's more peaceful with no stress involved. I put my head on his chest, and he rests his ultra-soft cheek on my head. Why does this position feel like it's meant to be?

The cute little girl from earlier comes running, asking me for a dance. Stephen looks at me with a loving stare as I pull away, granting her wish. I notice her eyes stay glued on my bracelet the entire time. My pastor once told me to share all that I can with the world around me. Now would be the perfect time to show some love to someone. I hand the little girl my beloved bracelet. It hurts a little to give away something I've loved for so long. But she's ecstatic, as if it's the most beautiful thing she has ever seen in her entire life. Coming to another country has opened up my eyes that others need help. They require love, real love. I feel the holy spirit nudging me to come back here in the future when I have more money to help.

As evening approaches, we head back to the cruise for some rest. On our way, Pablo calmly points out that a leech is attached to the back of my leg. I scream, shaking my leg in hopes of getting it off. Doing so does absolutely nothing. *Why do these things even exist?!* Quickly, Pablo tosses salt onto the blood-sucking leech. It lets go of my skin and dies. He picks it up, throwing it into the river for the fish to feast on.

"Eve, you must be careful when getting on and off the boat. Leeches like to stay in shallow water to grab onto their prey. Most people don't notice until it's too late," he warns.

Now that I think about it, I did accidentally put one leg into the river as I struggled to get on the boat. I've never dealt with such a problem in my years of being around the ocean and going fishing with my dad in different rivers. Good thing Pablo is an observant person.

"Yeah, Pablo, that could have been bad. Thank you," I say, annoyed at myself.

"Leeches aren't like regular bugs. They won't let go, no matter how much you wiggle them, scrape them off, or burn them. They only bite harder, making the wound take longer to heal. Sometimes, if you pull on them, their head can stay attached, biting your skin for weeks."

"Okay, I'll keep that in mind for next time."

Yuck. I am utterly disgusted by that leech; not only that, but it left a bite mark that still stings. I hop into the shower to get some relief. When bugs have mysteriously gotten on me, paranoia makes me feel that they are still there long after they are gone. One time, Sarah found a cockroach taking residence in my hair. A few days after a hurricane came through, we had no running water or electricity. Three days had gone by when Sarah and her parents came by to bring us some water. She randomly screamed, pointing at it. Her dad took it upon himself to get the creature out of my hair. I was so embarrassed for months. Then again, it would have been much worse if I had found it myself.

Pablo comes to my room to let me know that a special surprise is waiting in the lobby. Ecstatic, I stay in my pajamas and head to the lobby, into a special room, where I cannot believe my eyes.

CHAPTER 28

I walk up to a woman wearing a black chef-looking outfit without a tall, big hat. Candles lit up the room, releasing the aroma of different spices and flowers at the same time. The lights are dimmed to create a relaxing environment. I'm not too sure what's going on here, but it's definitely working on me.

"This massage is complementary." The woman stares at me with a huge smile. She must see right through me. Never in my entire life have I had the money to pay for something so luxurious. Lidia, the masseuse, prompts me toward a long chair where I need to lie on my belly. That posture can be uncomfortable and very vulnerable. This really does feel like a dream. Fear kicks in that it might be over in only a few days from now. How come when things are going well, there has to be an ending to it? In the world of Disney and fairy tales, the ending comes after the main story. Is happily ever after really a thing?

Instead of continuing to spiral, I think about all the good times in my life. Sarah, who saved me from the loneliness. My parents, who made me strong even when I didn't want to be. Christ, who has been here every step of the way, even when my life looked like chaos. Lidia works her magic through my shoulders, releasing all the tension from the last twenty-two years of my life.

All that Lucas ever did was hurt my self-identity. Any confidence I ever had was taken. He would joke about me looking like an old lady on my birthday, which I only get once every four years. Being born during a leap year isn't exactly as pleasant or cool as it seems to be. It truly does feel like it never comes. One time, in the third grade, our teacher decided to buy a cake and sing me the Happy Birthday song in front of everyone. It was heartwarming. It made me so happy that someone would do that for little me. Then Lucas had to destroy the positive moment. He screamed "Loser" in the background. People laughed at me. It was humiliating. Tears came flooding out at the thought of being stared at while laughing. Never will I understand how one person can ruin someone's life for that many years with no consequences. The teacher luckily sent him to a different classroom to be dealt with, but it was too late. When a moment is ruined, it's hard to remember it positively.

"Got a lot on your mind, don't you?" Lidia asks gently.

"How can you tell?" I am honestly curious.

"Your shoulders. They are extremely tense. It seems like you've never relaxed before."

She's right. Being on my own like this can be quite frightening. What's even scarier is having all these flashbacks throughout this trip. It's supposed to be a release. Instead, it's drawing me in deeper and deeper by the day. She lets me take a break to breathe. My muscles are already getting very sore. I go to the restroom to wash my face and give myself a pep talk that everything is going to be just fine. *My life is going to change.*

The massage continues. Lidia uses an amazing eucalyptus lotion for stress relief. She rubs so hard that another memory comes back to me of when Lucas threw a beehive at my back in the seventh grade. He and his friends joked about putting it in someone's shirt. I was caught in that mess. On my way to the vending machine during the break between classes, he ran up behind me and threw it lightly. It didn't necessarily hurt per se. But it was extremely alarming.

I wasn't expecting such a thing. The bees came out right away, stinging the back of my thigh and hip. I've never run that fast in my life. Lucas got punished with a suspension for an entire month. My parents almost pressed charges, but the principal convinced them that it was an accident. She had some kind of sweet spot for naughty children. Probably because of all he had been dealing with at home. The bee sting did not get infected as I wasn't allergic to them. But the fear of bugs just continued as he kept using it against me time and time again.

I feel a soothing release as if I've been in a hot tub. Next time, I'd like to get one of these with Sarah around so that my mind does not spiral. There's something about having a close friend nearby that makes things much easier. My grandma and I used to watch telenovelas, which are extremely dramatized Spanish shows. I became aware at a very young age that romantic relationships were way too dramatic. Friendships are more important to meet my needs and not be lonely. Having a good relationship with the creator of the universe plays a huge role as well.

I've never felt so relaxed and in control in my entire life. Lidia is amazing at this. I wonder where she learned how to do that. It's a job for the strong-willed, for those who enjoy helping other people feel relaxed. She did so well removing the tension from my muscles. Truthfully, there is always a lot on my mind, mostly about where my life has ended. I'm not that old, per se, but time does tick by. My job was supposed to lead me to greater victories and more money, hence leaving the apartment and eventually being able to afford to buy my own place. I never expected to be in the same exact position that I was when I first started working there. Becoming a manager or a financial advisor would have changed the trajectory of my life, but it didn't happen.

"You still seem deep in thought. Would you like some water?" Lidia reads my mind again.

Taking a break brings me back to reality. Everything is okay. Even if things don't go exactly as planned, maybe they were never meant to. I believe that God causes all things to happen for everyone's own good. I'm unsure how all these bad things that have happened to me were good for me, but only time will tell. Lidia returns with a scrumptious cup of water that I probably should have asked for half an hour ago. Interrupting her work was not an option.

"Okay, Eve, that is it for today. I hope you enjoyed it." She wipes off her sweat with a towel and helps me off the massage table with the other hand. She's probably exhausted by now. Time flew by, but it was indeed late at night, after all. I thank Lidia for all her hard work and effort. I wish I knew her personally; she seems like the type of person I'd want to have in my small friend circle. They'd love her so much. Especially with the possibility of receiving a discounted massage.

IN THE EARLY A.M., Stephen comes knocking on my door. I slept like a baby since all the muscle tension had been removed. Promising myself to look up a masseuse back in Miami, I open the door with a huge smile to see a sexy man waiting for me in the doorway. My eyes nearly bulge out of their sockets at the sight of him. He wears a tight tank top with cargo pants that make his thunder thighs glisten. I wonder what his behind looks like. *Hello, bubble butt.* A bandana hangs around his head, similar to a ninja. Probably to protect his gorgeous face from the monstrous sunbeams. Sunscreen isn't very popular here since everyone has skin that can withstand the heat. The trees here are tall and bushy enough to offer free natural shade that we don't have the luxury of in Florida. Trees tend to be maintained by the city to create a beach-like vibe.

"Eve, are you ready to go?" Stephen asks. He is so handsome. *Wow.*

"Where are we going this time?" The skin on my lip is sore and half bitten off from the number of times I've been nervous and flirty over the past few days.

I feel an overwhelming sense of being seen. No one has ever made me feel this way. Stephen's gaze is steady, locking onto mine with an intensity that makes my heart race. Yesterday, when we danced, my chest pressed tightly against his. Every moment felt electric. How exhilarating it is to be embraced with so much love. Being caught in the moment like that makes everything else fade away.

"We are going fishing for something a little different," he smirks.

Do I dare ask what he means by that? Nope. I'm way too busy admiring his face and muscles. I grab my bag and head to the lobby, a little nervous about what could possibly be going down today. Pablo waits for us both to wake up so that we can head out. The boat required a few holes to be patched up anyway. I notice that Pablo already has the fishing poles ready. Someone is excited to go fishing. My dad would love this.

"Is there anything I can help with? I don't mind putting the bait on," I ask, hoping to get some attention from Stephen.

Maybe I can play dumb so that he'll teach me and come closer to me. Although that tactic never exactly worked for me before. I once had a crush on a guy named Ben, who seemed to be one of the coolest people at school. Little did I know that he had been good friends with Lucas. Before finding that out, we had a math class together, geometry, which required a specific skill set to pass the class. He was somewhat smart. Always answering all the teacher's questions. I kind of admired how he had a love for math. I tried to play dumb multiple times, asking for his help with a specific math question in hopes of getting to know him better. Those math problems were actually a piece of cake to me since my dad taught me how to do math when I was little.

Ben ended up making a few mistakes, which led me to the wrong answer. Holding back was nearly impossible. My love for math couldn't let it go. He did not take it well that he had been wrong. One thing led to another, creating a huge barrier between us. It turned out he didn't like Hispanic girls anyway. At least that's what Lucas rubbed in my face the very next day. He told me I was too ugly to even consider dating a guy like Ben, who only was passionate about girls with blond hair and blue eyes. Being a cheerleader was also a requirement. I never in my life wanted that kind of attention. Never have and never will.

"Sure! If you don't mind," Pablo responds, surprised. "Stephen, son, help her put those on. They wiggle and jump a lot."

Wait. Jump? *What did I just get myself into?* Stephen brings out a massive, smelly bucket. With fear of looking down, I open one eye. They're grasshoppers. Live ones. I can hear squirming and lots of movement. Some of them attempt to jump to their freedom. The bucket has a thin layer of netting on top. That way, none of them can successfully escape. They came in all sizes, shapes, and colors. Most of them were either lime green or dark brown, with the exception of a few illuminating a blue-yellow glow.

"Uh, how do we do this?" I loathe to ask.

"Like this. Follow my lead," Stephen answers compassionately.

It is comforting to see how nonchalant he is around critters. It doesn't faze him at all. Taking the hook in one hand, he dunks his hand into the filthy, bug-infested bucket, bringing out one of the brown ones. It swirls for its life, even trying to fly away. Stephen punctures its little body with the tip of the hook, making sure that the creature stays secure. With all the might of his strong biceps, he flings the grasshopper as far as he possibly can into the water. Seconds turn into minutes when a fish takes hold of the grasshopper. The fish nearly pulls the entire fishing pole into the water when Stephen fights with all his might. Reeling it in to see the final result, the fish escapes with the bait as its prize. The look of disappointment on Stephen's face is heartbreaking.

"You see, that's the thing about fishing. It is a gamble. There is no right or wrong way to do it. Only getting the principles correct will save you much time." Pablo lets out a big laugh.

Driving the boat is like clockwork for Pablo. He turns the engine on and takes us to a different spot. With it being their main point of transportation from island to island, the boat is in great condition. I secretly plan on giving him a large tip along with a fantastic Google review. People need to experience this. The river is as beautiful as ever—brown, yet it has so much charm. It doesn't smell or seem contaminated in any way. The people utilize this river. They take care of it. It is the heart of their well-being.

The engine comes to a stop. Stephen lowers the tiny anchor, signifying that we are here at the mysterious place. The cruise is a little far away, but it is nice to finally get an excursion not involving too many other people. Being the introvert that I am, I prefer to be around a small circle that doesn't require too much out of me. Saving my energy is a must.

"Here, Eve, this one is for you." Stephen hands me the nicest fishing pole out of the three. It makes me feel bad. The wooden rod contains carvings with cute little symbols all around. They remind me of ancient markings found in caves. I watched the Discovery Channel a ton when I was a little girl. My papa knew that it was a great way to release stress.

The fishing poles all have unique designs. Mine just happens to be the largest. I ask Stephen to show me one more time how to put the bait on the hook. My hands tremble, causing the first two to fly away to safety. I grab one of the pretty blue-yellow ones. It has to be held super tightly in order to put it onto the hook. Not knowing the best place to puncture it, I place the hook into its legs. *Yes, finally, I've done it.* Who cares about checking for security? I'm throwing this sucker! I launch it straight into the water closest to the boat. My hands go numb. Stephen nods at me with a smile. He is pleased. Mission accomplished.

"That's it, keep it up!" Pablo praises me. It feels good. I can now conquer the world!

Suddenly, something begins to bite. It isn't that strong of a force, but it still makes me nervous. After a second, I start to reel in when Stephen comes behind me to assist. *Am I dreaming right now?* His chest presses fully onto my back; he grabs the pole, moving it to a sharp left to get the fish hooked. We reel it in together in sync. A disgusting, alien-looking fish with large teeth appears. No way. It's a piranha.

"What you are seeing here is a local delicacy," Pablo explains. "After descaling it, we season it with garlic, herbs, jalapeño, and a little bit of ginger. Then, we light the fire and fry it in a boiling pot of oil, making the skin very crispy. My wife is the best at this."

"Oh, I'm so excited to try it. Can we do that today?" I beg.

"Hmm, maybe," he hesitates. He obviously has a different agenda.

Stephen takes hold of the bucket to prepare the remainder of the bait. The disgust on my face gives it away that I truly don't want to continue stabbing these poor, mindless grasshoppers to death. He is the type of guy who lives by actions, not words. He gets me.

Pablo goes at it, releasing his line into the river like a professional. Piranhas travel together in packs, looking for their next victim. The fish that terrorizes humans in multiple Hollywood films is nowhere near cute. Glowing with two shades of colors—blue and orange—the red eyes look evil. Native to South America for over three million years, they are known as carnivores that devour human flesh within minutes. What a high reputation to withhold. Pablo tells me that they mostly eat bugs, worms, seeds, plant material, and random small mammals that come too close to the water if the fish is starving.

Stephen outdid us all. Five fish flop onto the boat one after the other. They are stored inside a cooler full of ice. He definitely has skill, but one thing is for certain: Pablo held back. I know he only wants to see his son thrive and to make him shine. *How sweet.*

"How the heck did you catch so many?" I grumble.

"I fish every day," he says proudly.

I would be, too. Life in the Amazon doesn't consist of too many activities. The locals mostly chill at home with their families or participate in their trade of experience. Children are tasked with climbing trees to get coconuts, while moms spend their time weaving clothes or tending to their vegetable gardens. The husbands are more concerned with making sure their farm animals are taken care of. Bringing meat to the table can be daunting.

"Eve, what do you like to do during your spare time?" Pablo implores.

"Uh, that's a hard question. When I'm not pushing myself with the frustrations at work, I get lost in dancing," I giggle. "My friends are also super fun to be around."

Oh, how I miss them. James will be the first to ask a million questions about how things went. Traveling would check off one item on his bucket list. More importantly, landing a major deal with an organization for his designs would be life-changing. Drawing, painting, and designing all in one could beat going around the world in a heartbeat for James. Someday, he and Elizabeth will finally tie the knot. Their personalities differ greatly, yet opposites do attract in most cases. I've heard it causes much tension. At the same time, it sounds like tons of fun.

The wind blows absurdly strong, and I know it's time to head back. Rainstorms happen daily around certain times of the day, some stronger than others. Rocking back and forth, the boat becomes uncontrollable. Pablo attempts to hold us in place with the paddle, but it is too strong.

"Hold on tight!" Pablo warns.

It's cold. I open my eyes, but the water is too murky to see. Shadows appear next to me. *Oh no, are these the piranhas?* Curiosity brings them in closer. It isn't enough to smell my fear in the depths of the shallow water. Standing up doesn't occur to me. The brown kelp at the river floor catches my feet, locking me in place. This is the end. I'm going to be mangled by fish. Suddenly, a larger shadow descends. Its face is unrecognizable and blurry. Maybe it's an angel.

CHAPTER 29

*T*he angel pulls me up on the boat. My brain flakes out, not understanding what just happened. All I know is that I was supposed to be dead, mauled by angry piranhas trying to take revenge for hurting their brothers and sisters. Instead of devouring my flesh for violating their home, they stood by, watching me. They did not go insane the way movies portray them.

"Eve, here." Stephen removes his shirt, exposing all the muscles I'd been staring at the entire day. He wraps the shirt around me, bringing me in close to suck up his warmth. The lack of words or the ability to think is intriguing. I could have died, but there is no time to think. I rest in the arms of the one who risked his own life to save mine. Silence overcomes us.

"Ouch," I wince. A small scrape stings on my shin.

"Oh no. Let's head back to the village. Laurinda can help." Pablo frets.

In total, eight fish were captured to be eaten tonight. Five of those were caught by Stephen, two by Pablo, and only one by me, which Stephen assisted me with. Pablo must have planned on cooking them in the cruise ship kitchen. There is a large enough space to support all their guests. To my surprise, we press forward in waters that look familiar. Sloths stare me down from the trees, threatening not to get near their baby. Its skin appears smooth to the touch. Probably as fluffy as a cat. I'm not about to test this theory, though, as I don't want to anger the family of sloths.

As the boat reaches the island's shore, Pablo dashes toward the village in search of help. A few men come out to help lift me when Stephen tells them he will handle it. He promises to carry me to safety. The man has done so much for me already, but I enjoy it too much to protest.

Into a hut, Stephen dunks his head, placing me on a square mat made out of bamboo. The hardness makes the pain in my leg easier to forget about. I have the soreness from the previous night of intense massaging to thank for it. My hair makes the situation worse since it's dripping cold water. An old woman with the scent of spices and herbs greets me with a warm smile. Remaining calm becomes easy after sensing her kind vibes. She passes me a cup with beautiful, unique lettering on it. The golden handle reveals the age of the teacup. All scratched up and dented, and it probably has been used on many patients before me. Blissful flowers melt inside my mouth as I take a large gulp of the warm tea.

"Eve, this is Laurinda. She will patch up your wound now," Pablo says in distress.

Cleaning the cut produces a sharp, stinging pain that lingers slightly worse than a paper cut. Those small cuts pack a punch compared to the much larger ones that require a hospital visit and stitches. I nearly pass out from shock, but having Stephen next to me makes it all worth it. A light-yellow liquid called jojoba oil is poured all over my leg. A shiver runs down my spine. My mom uses this method to soothe her eczema. Natural oils have multiple healing properties, like relieving pain, reducing inflammation, preventing scarring, and helping the overall healing process.

"Medicine," Laurinda mentions, not knowing that I've seen this method used before. I appreciate her honesty. She tries her best to speak the little English she knows, but ends up utilizing Stephen for assistance when she struggles.

"Got it, thanks," I weep.

"Ela precisa de descanso." Laurinda beams at Stephen, who isn't leaving my side for even a second. I won't allow it. *No way.*

"She says that you require rest for the medicine to take effect," Stephen expresses.

"Where are you going? Please don't leave me," I beg.

"Okay, okay. I will stay until you fall asleep."

Stephen stays with me the entire time, as promised, although falling asleep isn't an option. I cannot fathom the fact that my life was almost over in an instant. Why did the piranhas not attack me? Instead of worrying too much, I remember what the masseuse told me last night, that I need to stop holding in so much tension. It must be released if I want to be healed.

"Hey, Stephen?" I ask.

"Yes, Eve?" he counters.

"Why didn't the piranhas destroy me when I fell?"

"Ah, uh, hard to explain. Let me get Pai." Stephen makes his way towards the door, looking me in the eyes, telling me not to move an inch.

"I've heard that you've got some questions?" Pablo comes into the room as sad as can be. I've never seen such a horrid look on his face.

"Yes, but first, what's the matter?"

Taking the spot by my side, he weeps, cradling his face. "I just... feel so much shame."

"Pablo, none of this is your fault. Please. I had tons of fun catching those little monsters. Plus, I got to overcome a piece of my fear of touching bugs, thanks to you." I rub his shoulder as I would have done to my own father. "Nothing bad happened. I'm still here, alive and well."

"I'm so, so sorry."

"Don't sweat it, I promise. This is a moment I'll remember forever," I say. "Now, I want to know. Why did those piranhas not devour my flesh?"

"The reason is that you did not make a peep after getting engulfed. The other reason is that piranhas only eat large creatures that are dead, if they are starving. Only small live animals and bugs interest them."

"Ah, I see. So, I was never a target to begin with. But why did they watch me?"

"Piranhas only attack if you get anywhere near their eggs. They were watching to make sure you weren't going to hurt them."

"What about the scrape on my leg? Does it look like a piranha chomp to you?" I joke, but Pablo takes it seriously, not understanding my sense of humor.

"No, no. It's from falling out of the boat."

"If I got cut before getting into the water, is it possible that the piranhas were attracted to the scent of it?"

"It is possible. But the fact that they didn't do anything is truly a miracle," he says with glowing eyes, wiping away the left-over tears. "Camila, my wife, is making a delicious dinner for us. Feel better soon. Get some rest."

I lay my head on the rock-hard bamboo mat with no pillow. A change of clothes is brought to me from one of the villagers who is worried sick. Everyone living here has the most genuine heart. They are the kindest people I've ever met. I hear someone slip out of the tent slowly and quietly. Looking over at him with one eye open, I decide to leave him be. Stephen watched over me for the past few hours. He has stuff to do, probably.

"Eve, Eve, wake up." I recognize that voice immediately, but my mind struggles to place it. Am I dreaming? I open my eyes to a blurry, beautiful face looking at me with an adorable smile. It's Stephen, his voice gently coaxing me back to reality.

"Are you able to walk?" he asks, concern etching his brow. The heaviness of sleep still clings to me. I can't tell if I'm strong enough or if it's going to be painful. I feel the cold dampness of my shirt, where drool drips from my face. *Gross.* How long have I been asleep? The room spins as I try to focus on his gaze.

One muscle at a time, I extend my good leg forward to hold myself up. Stephen positions himself next to me in the rare event that I pummel down to the ground. The bad leg has zero motivation to move. *Great.* But my stomach makes all the decisions around here.

Stephen leads me to the family campfire. "Here is your plate," he says with those big brown, loving eyes. I could kiss him right now for saving my life.

My cheeks get all flustered as we eat silently, enjoying the marvelous creation on the plate. The mouth of the piranha is cut out. I wonder what the teeth looked like. The skin, fried to a crisp, is so delicious. It tastes normal, like tilapia. No one would ever know that this was the carnivorous creature everyone is terrified of because of all the movies that misrepresent them. Lemon was sprinkled all over the fish, creating a citrus effect, though it was not needed since Camila did an amazing job already. I wish that I had any kind of skill in cooking. She took the few ingredients she had on hand to make such a delicacy shine so brightly. It is one ugly-looking fish. I'm not even going to lie.

This practice of gathering as a family around the campfire and sharing fish with the neighbors next door happens here on a weekly basis. The village girls perform a dance for entertainment since there are no electronics. The beating of the drums forces my head to start a slow bob. Stephen watches me to make sure my leg is okay. My belly is too full to handle anything else. What a day it has been.

Laurinda comes by to check in on how my scrape is doing and puts more medication on it. She gives me an unexpected bear hug. "Boa noite," she says. It sounds similar to goodnight in Spanish. I knew knowing Spanish would eventually come in handy someday, although I only speak it when the situation calls for it. Portuguese sounds so beautiful. The way it comes out with a slur is similar to Italian. The accent is very attractive.

My leg hurts when I walk, but it's tolerable enough to move forward today. My belly tingles at the thought of seeing Stephen, my hero.

The next morning, I awaken feeling groggy, with boogers crusted around my eyes, after being confined to bed rest last night. A few elders from the village come over to the hut to see me and sing prayers over me. No one has ever done this for me before. Laurinda puts her hand on my shoulder, giving me a big smile and kissing my forehead. It feels like I got her blessing.

"Thank you, guys! I'm feeling much better!" I exclaim.

I go outside to see everyone waiting for me, being super cheerful. They give me huge hugs, including the cutest toddlers, who couldn't join in the dancing celebration last night since it was past their bedtime. They aren't cranky at all and look well-fed.

"Good morning, Eve! We're heading to the market today," Pablo says, looking super happy to see me. I could get used to this feeling. Being loved by a tribe is precious.

"Oh, okay. Yes. I would love to see where your village does their shopping," I respond, honored to be invited, although it's what I paid to do.

"Do you feel okay to walk?"

"It still hurts, but I can walk perfectly fine."

"We'll take it slow; I promise."

Stephen sneaks behind me, drenching me with his hugs. A

long hug that makes everyone stare and smile even bigger. I don't care; this is the best part of my day. My cheeks are hot. Pablo sends an angry look towards Stephen, but he doesn't let go.

"I wanted to thank you for, er, saving me." I rub the back of my head.

"Any time." Stephen blushes.

We hop onto the small boat, this time with Camila. She needs to buy more ingredients and thread to sew a project she's been working on for the past few months. Time is endless here. Hobbies can be pursued because there aren't any social pressures to be at a certain spot in life. Stephen's entire family is made of amazing, flawless people. His mom hugs me tightly, rubbing my back for comfort. She knows I am in distress, but not for the reason everyone probably thinks. The scrape doesn't bother me, and neither does the incident from yesterday. What truly is hurting me is the fact that in a few days, I'll be leaving this marvelous place.

Seafood, seafood, seafood everywhere! Most of the food stalls showcase ingredients found only in the Amazon, turning them into local delicacies. One of the vendors sells all kinds of fruits. Perfectly shaped watermelons, papaya, small bananas, jalapeños, avocados, you name it. Camila feasts her eyes on all the foods she has been wanting for the past month. The villagers only go shopping once a month due to increased inflation rates. Buying as much as the boat can handle is a way of saving money. I'd be surprised if the boat didn't sink. We'll see how good that little boat really is, I guess.

Pablo and his wife return to the boat to unload all the merchandise that they bought while Stephen and I continue with the exploration. Clothing displays are completely different here. White mannequins stare us down with their blank faces. No lipstick or anything. They do have wigs with different hair colors and styles, along with hats. Outfit by outfit, I see a few that interest me. Right next to the stall, a gang of motorcycles waits to be loved on, their bright colors gleaming in the sunlight. I stand mesmerized, envisioning Stephen sweeping me up on a fast, powerful bike as we race toward the home of our dreams. *What am I thinking?!*

The vendors at the food stalls are very respectful. They don't yell at people to come buy their food like some of the food trucks and stalls at the fair back home. Going to the mall can be extremely annoying. Paid employees would stand right in front of the store to attract buyers, pressuring them to come in. I feel bad looking in the other direction to avoid their gaze. Sometimes, they'd make a noise or try to engage in conversations, and I couldn't hold back from being nice even though my conscience told me, "Run, now!"

"Eve, does anything look good to you?" Stephen asks lovingly.

"Everything is amazing. It's such a hard choice. What do you recommend?"

He gives me a blank stare, unsure how to respond. The last thing I want to do is push him too much when English is already tough. It is said to be one of the hardest languages to learn when it isn't your first language. I believe it. English is weird sometimes, plus it is infused with French words that make no sense. It's spelled one way but said another.

Stephen walks over to a food stall to get something. I stay put since I don't want to embarrass him if the vendor were to speak to me. Not knowing the local language can be difficult, but it does provide a moment to breathe without feeling nervous.

"Try this." Stephen hands me a freezing cup with a tiny wooden spoon.

"Thank you. Is this ice cream?" I ask curiously.

"*CupuaVu* cream."

Not sure what to expect, I lift a spoonful of the creamy,

milk-like substance into my mouth. The fragrance of pineapple mixed with melon blesses my nostrils. My tongue feels the milk sticking to it. The fresh, earthy flavors, along with a soft yet solid texture, are so delicious.

"Mmm, this is so good!" I exclaim. It's been a couple of weeks since I've binged on any ice cream. Without any sadness or stress, there hasn't been any reason to. My dentist is going to love this new trend. Every time I get my teeth cleaned, she can tell if I went to bed the night before without brushing.

Stephen, who is pleased with my reaction to the delicious dessert, drags me to a shady area underneath a tree. Good thing he did, my skin has always been the sensitive type. James would be thanking him right now if he were currently here. Oh, how I wish I could grab a spoonful and feed it to Stephen. But what if he thinks that's weird? I'm not sure if that is culturally accepted, especially since my germs are spread all over the spoon. But this is the opportunity to do something spontaneous, since Pablo isn't around to flash a funny look.

"Would you like to try some?" I ask hesitantly.

"No, no. I have had it all my life," he says, "you go ahead and enjoy it."

Aw, man. Is he sure, though? I press on anyway. "But Stephen, this one is completely different than the ones you've tasted."

Success. He gives in to my pressure. I grab a spoonful, launching it in his direction towards his beautiful, soft lips. My hands wobble when, finally, his lips come apart, accepting the gesture. I close my eyes in fear of being too embarrassed. He clasps my hand, giving me the most satisfying look. I blush, happy that I took the chance.

CHAPTER 30

*W*hen Stephen and I returned to the boat yesterday, we found Pablo and Camila hugging and giggling together. It was the cutest thing I've ever seen. Parents should always be in love and maintain that even after their children grow into adulthood. My parents tolerate each other, for the most part, and they don't really try to be all romantic anymore. It's comforting to see Stephen's parents still having that deep connection in their older age.

Our adventure today entails traveling to the mainland to attend a botanical garden. The magnificent garden is magical. The birds are locked up in large enclosures, yet look free. The garden is a haven for a few animals, but it mostly houses different protected bug species.

"Shall we?" I blush at Steven, opening the front door so that he can go inside before me. In all honesty, I want to check out his behind. His back muscles are exposed in his tank top. Pablo sees me do this but doesn't say a word about it, thank goodness. I don't want him to assume that I'm seducing his son. The employees handling the garden are extremely welcoming, providing us with a map of the entire garden along with a description of each animal. Luckily, there are signs with different descriptions for plant life.

According to the sign, bananas share half of their genetic material with humans. *Wow, that's amazing.* One of the plants is called a howler monkey tail, known for its stem that is smothered in orange scales, giving it a hairy appearance. I reach out to get a feel of the texture. My hand withdraws at the touch of something hairy. I've never seen most of the plants here. Another plant has orange dots all over the bottom side. It looks like little bugs trying to suck away all of the nutrients. They typically grow in sandy areas like Brazil and Mexico. Many different plants prefer to be in a moist area on the canopy floor or underneath other trees that prevent the sunlight from burning them. The growth of plants in this way promotes the overgrowth of certain species. Like bugs or rodents, some plants are considered invasive and can pose a massive problem.

Pablo tells me that there is a lady in the village who is a botanist. She can grow anything with the right soil and a seed. When a plant starts to wither, she is called to find the problem and help fix it. At times, it could be lacking sunlight, taking in way too much water, or there may not be enough nutrients in the soil. Ana has given great advice to all the farmers on the island for many years so that the village may thrive off its vegetables and fruits.

A plant with a large red bulb, that looks like dragon fruit, catches my attention. The sign mentions that the name is roselle, originating from Africa. For years, it has been used to make hibiscus tea. Its leaves can be consumed in different variations of salads. Slaves used it as food. I wonder if there would be a way to try it, though not the one in front of me, of course; that would be a violation of garden rules. Sadness fills my heart at the thought of slavery in history. All the injustices that had been done to others.

"Eve, this section over here contains all the different fruits, herbs, spices, and medicines used in the Amazon," Pablo explains proudly, pointing at a few found in the village.

A prickly plant called achiote can be used to make medicine, paint, and cosmetics. The process of extracting the pigment is tedious. Only someone skilled in the craft may have a crack at it. I bet Laurinda knows how. Pupunha, a fruit cooked in salt water, is often consumed by the locals on very hot days. Peppercorn plants can be found everywhere in the country. According to the description, it was once the most valuable kitchen condiment in the world. Brazil has been the top producer and exporter of it.

A sensitive fern is said to shy away when being touched. I decide to test the theory. The plant crunches up immediately within itself, looking sad. I can't help but laugh at this. Marveling at such a plant, Stephen looks at me tenderly. I showed my true colors in front of him, the silly, childish nature that does not have a wall put up. I wish I could be this way all the time, but I only can be when no one is around. It's a defense mechanism. The fear that Lucas has placed in my life is very hard to get rid of.

The final plant produces a red to deep purple fruit that, when opened, reveals a bright orange or dark yellow interior. It's a shrub that naturally grows in backyard gardens. Locals use them to prepare jams, juices, fish, and chicken. What an amazing experience to be able to go outside and find all the fruits and vegetables needed to cook a decent meal. It would prevent having to go to the store and get tempted by the way that professional marketers set it up. Consumers are essentially being tricked into buying things they don't need. For me, it's always the chocolate bar section right in front of the register. Sometimes, the line will take so long, forcing me to look around at more items in the area. It takes practice and dedication to say no when my stomach keeps telling me yes.

Up ahead, there's a spot that houses a few native species of fish. I see a gray, spotted fish staring my way. He has whiskers and cute pink fins. The sign called it a pirarucu. It is very similar to a catfish. There is a well-known story that mentions that the fish occasionally rise in the water to get a breath of fresh air. Each fish has a different sound when it comes to the surface. Villagers sometimes know which one took its last breath.

"Hey, Pablo, are there any of these fish near the village?" I ask.

"Yes, there is an area nearby, away from the piranha-infested waters," Pablo says.

"Do you think we can go there today to see them?"

"Yes. I'll have Stephen take you there this afternoon before dark."

An electrical eel gazes, looking like an ancient dinosaur, not like the ones in the movies. It contains its own bio-batteries that recharge. When the eel feeds, it electrifies its prey in order to devour it. The angelfish are a lot more understanding. It simply roams around, utilizing its freedom within the tank. It's amazing the creations that God has made. Each with their own unique personality. He didn't create one to be a certain way; instead, they forge the way themselves. With people, it's the same way. We're all meant for great things, but it's so easy to get caught up comparing ourselves on social media or even to our own family.

The next exhibit contains local indigenous tribal wear and different art sculptures. Many of the locals cannot afford vaccines or don't believe in them. When foreigners come by, they are against it. People get sick and don't have the antibodies to fight infections or viruses. There used to be six million indigenous people. Unfortunately, those numbers have decreased significantly to 300 thousand living in the Amazon rainforest. The artwork signified multiple tragedies. The defor-estation of their home has left a tremendous imprint. Rivers became contaminated with mercury from excessive mining and toxicants. Stephen wears a disgruntled frown with his lower lip pushed out. It's clear that he feels sad for his people. I place my hand on his shoulder.

"Hey, Stephen, I know this is hard for you. It's going to be okay," I say, teary-eyed.

"Yeah, you're right," he responds.

"Things will get better with time."

"How do you know?

"I put my faith in God, knowing that he will bring justice to all those who are oppressed. I, too, have had my fair share of that battle."

He pulls me in for a warm embrace. It's nice when someone can understand how you're feeling. Although my family has never been treated unfairly in the same way, I personally felt hatred from other people for no reason. Mom told me when I was little to be strong yet meek. To this day, I never understood how to do both. Kindness overtakes my strength, sucking it all away into the deep abyss. People like to take that and abuse it. History is repeated over and over again—the strong taking advantage of the weak.

Trying to shake off thoughts of violence from history, we head toward the prized section—the real reason we came to this botanical garden: to look at bugs. All kinds of creepy critters are on display, from jumping spiders to gorgeous native butterflies. The entire lifecycle of a butterfly, from start to finish, is right in front of my eyes. Cute little green caterpillars eat many leaves to their heart's desire, ready for the next stage—getting into their cocoon. Becoming a butterfly is the accomplished goal of a caterpillar, along with making babies to ensure the next generation has a chance in life. Most females only mate shortly after emerging.

The spider exhibit is quite unique, displaying spiders I've never laid eyes on. One is shaped like a heart. It could be mistaken for a fruit if it were any bigger. I have to admire the spider's courage. Even when they see people coming, they stay put in the middle of their web, waiting for a bug to stop by. Another one of the spiders stares at me with deep intent. I'm so fortunate that humans cannot actually be eaten by one. Its body reminds me of a demon. At least it doesn't have eight different eyes like a tarantula.

"Eve, do you want to hold one of the friendly spiders?" Pablo jokes.

"Uh, no thanks," I spit out.

Being able to look at them without getting grossed out is good enough in my book. I even went as far as to touch grasshoppers. Don't even get me started on touching a spider that can actually cause harm. I am still too afraid of being bitten and having to rush to Laurinda since the hospital is too far away. It's better to be safe than sorry.

As promised, Stephen brings me alone on the small boat to go see the fish that come up to breathe for air. They really did make a funny, distinct sound when coming up to the surface. The anchor is dropped in a spot not too close to the fish, or else they'd get too scared. Camila packed some pillows onto the boat so that our butts wouldn't hurt sitting out here watching them. She made sure to give Stephen a warning not to keep me out here too late past dark. Anyway, fish typically sleep when the sun goes down.

I overheard Pablo talking to his son, advising him not to get too close to me, as I will be leaving soon. A reminder that I am a foreigner who shouldn't be pushing my luck. It hurts too much to think that I might not ever see Stephen again. He has made me so happy—the happiest I've been in a very long time.

He sits next to me, putting his arm around my shoulder as we watch the fish come up. What bliss. His chest is nice and comfy to lie on. I can't help but feel up his biceps. *What am I doing?* Oh well. We're already caught up in the moment, snuggling. I adore everything about the village. How well they take care of their people, and especially the way everyone shares food and knowledge. Different trades are utilized to function as their own mini-society. Even though the village is not technologically advanced, it's more peaceful than anywhere I've ever been.

Suddenly, Amora pounces from the bushes onto the tree above us. Stephen's eyes light up, and he immediately invites her over. There is no way she could land on the boat without falling into the water. She must have been waiting for Stephen to come out and play with her, as he does a couple of times per week. Amora relies on him for snacks and love.

"Will you ever tell your dad about Amora?" I ask.

"No, never. He wouldn't let me see her ever again." Stephen sighs.

"I see. Is there a way to prove to him that she's friendly?"

"He doesn't like associating with wild animals. It isn't in our culture to do it. There are conservation laws that prevent this also."

I know Stephen wishes that Amora could live as a pet in the village. They would probably never allow it. It looks like there are things that are frowned upon here, too. Unwritten rules that prevent people from doing certain things.

"In the U.S., people are allowed to have pets with some limitations. If the animal is endangered, then it is frowned upon and could produce a large fine," I explain.

"Oh. Would they accept Amora?" he asks.

"Uh, honestly, probably not."

CHAPTER 31

*J*n the morning, I am offered a pineapple martini, which I gladly accept. Drinking doesn't usually interest me, especially after the one time I let myself get carried away. The night was spent over the toilet with Sarah holding my hair. All I remember is the disgusting pineapple flavor mixed in with the alcohol. This martini is completely different, though. It doesn't leave a bad taste in my mouth. Only sweetness with a pinch of a sting. My mom always says that experiences need to happen for one to grow, even the bad ones. Too much alcohol that day was a necessary evil that made me more conscious of potential issues if I were to overdose. Back then, it was a cool thing to do. It has no power over me now.

"Ola, bom dia, Eve!" Pablo surprises me.

"Oh, hi guys, good morning!" I reply with an annoyed, sleepy tone.

Stephen blows me a kiss when his father isn't looking. Ever since that moment I got hurt while fishing, he's been acting extremely sweet. Actually, the entire time I've been here. When he looks at me with those deep brown eyes, it makes me never want to leave this place. He pats my head as if I'm a five-year-old, making my cheeks burn hot. It's embarrassing to feel the way I do without being able to communicate effectively.

Instead of going to another island, the small boat takes us on a few loops to see the sights better. The boat driver points out a few pink dolphins that are jumping in and out of the water. They have no care in the world. A sloth stares right into my soul from up above, deep in the trees. I can tell they're sick of seeing random people since we are a threat to their environment. Luckily, the locals are extremely respectful when they explore the forest. We are constantly told to keep our voices down when passing different wildlife, as they should not be disturbed.

The boat comes to a halt near a different part of the forest. No path has been made. It is uninhabited. Only trees, animals, and rain. That's the way I like it. There's more of a sense of adventure, not knowing where we are going. Stephen disembarks from the small boat and walks toward me, his arm reaching out. I am flattered. He helps me out without a scratch. Not like before, I would get out of the boat and get my boot stuck in the mud. *No leeches today.* A group of other tourists tags along for the excursion. Many different perspectives are being expressed. It's annoying. One guy mentions that he hasn't been eating since he got here for fear of getting sick from contaminated food. Another lady tells me that she got to hug a baby sloth. I feel instant jealousy. Although I'm truly here for a bug experience. There are so many marvelous creatures.

My boots become muddy and slippery, almost dangerous. I daydream of falling into a mud pit and having Stephen carry me the rest of the way. I could hop onto his strong back while he held onto my thighs. Back to reality, I step on a dead earthworm and hear the crunch. *Oh, yuck. Why me?* From the corner of my eye, I can see others also getting disgusted by the amount of mud and getting soaked from the rain that randomly started. My hair is covered in sweat, muck, and rain. My mom once told me that it's unsafe to be out in the rain. It can make you sick with a fever. But wait, if I get a fever, does that mean I can stay a little longer with Stephen? *Oh my. Why am I thinking this way?* I have a mission to complete. The goal is to get rid of my fear of bugs. I start walking quickly to catch up with Pablo.

"Hey Pablo, where are we going?" I ask to distract myself from my own thoughts.

"You'll have to wait and see. It's another surprise." He winks.

"I don't like surprises."

The hike treks on, although some people got trapped in mud with trees whipping as we attempt to squeeze through tight areas. The way up is quite steep, but doesn't stop the excitement of going to the surprise location that Pablo did a great job at keeping hush about. The bugs stick around, even in the midst of a small rainstorm. Gnats fly around my head, enjoying my suffering. Stephen peeks back at me to make sure that I'm keeping up with the rest of the group. My sandal gets caught on a rock, and I almost stumble to the ground. Luckily, we are all walking close enough to each other to make sure no one is left behind by accident. It would be a huge problem to get lost without a path to follow or a way to get back. Not to mention, there's no phone reception.

Out of breath, sweaty, and soaked from the rain, we make it to the very top. I didn't bother drinking water. I cannot miss the beauty in front of my eyes. *Amazing!* The sound of running water is so loud that I can't talk to Pablo or the person behind me. Raccoon-looking creatures come out in a big hurdle to beg for food. The temptation to feed the poor little creatures gets stumped when I notice signs everywhere warning tourists not to feed the animals. There must be a valid reason for this. I follow my gut and hold back from doing so. I hear a loud "Ouch!" behind me. The leader of the group scolds the man for not paying attention to the signs that are posted in English everywhere. People really are dense.

We head towards the edge of the waterfall. The drop looks

utterly terrifying, but luckily, Stephen stands right behind me. The water blasts with pressure. The panorama of multiple waterfalls makes it seem like a dream. The sound of the water can put anyone to sleep with how relaxing it is. I get closer to the edge, where the water falls at a faster rate. The splashes and steam of the water soak my clothes even more. It's cold, but it feels so good after that long hike up.

Never have I been the type who enjoys exercising or even going on hikes. Mostly because of the bugs that fly around while being sweaty. Gnats, bees, and mosquitoes infest every forest in Miami, especially the Everglades. It's the only place where humans have not tried to build houses and businesses. Bug spray makes my skin welt and smell like poison. Instead of dealing with all of this, I just avoid going outside unless I am going to a body of water.

Exercise is a huge part of staying alive longer. It's extremely necessary but not practiced nearly as much as it should. Except for bodybuilders. Honestly, the sight of those guys makes me nauseous. The amount of work they put in is tremendous and respectable. I've heard that in Japan, sumo wrestlers put in similar amounts of work. Lots of eating is needed to be strong enough to face their opponents. The main goal is to become the greatest of them all, a Yokozuna.

A lot of the other tourists who came on this excursion are very large. The amazement of the waterfall doesn't help the fact that most of them are gasping to have a drink of water. The majority of humans in the world are out of shape.

Birds fly gracefully over us. Large beaks in all kinds of colors. That's when I realize they're toucans! *How beautiful.* They apparently travel in pairs during the mating season. The male bird is always the larger, more colorful one. From the distance and the splashes from the waterfall, a grand rainbow appears, which is a reminder of God's promise to never flood the Earth again.

"Beautiful, right?" Stephen comes close to me.

"Yes, very," I say with hot cheeks again.

He reaches out to grab hold of my hand. I let him because why not? He intertwines his fingers with mine, noticing I have a very small hand. I want to do this forever. Nothing can ruin this moment, well, except Pablo.

"Hey, love birds, we must be going. It's starting to get dark. We have to get back," he reminds us of what he told us back in the village. I'm sick of hearing it.

"Can't we stay a little longer?" I beg.

He chuckles with a huge smile. Everyone starts moving again down the sloped mountain. The way down is a lot harder than the way up because my toes keep smashing against my sandals. If I'd known there was going to be a hike involved, I would have brought better shoes before leaving this morning. The sun looks marvelous during sunset. Bright red, yellow, and orange engulf the sky until it's no more.

"Look at this, everyone," says one of the tour guides.

He points at a tree that seems to be infested with worms. My heart sinks as I notice Stephen grabbing one and walking towards me with it. *Oh no.*

"This is called a dragon caterpillar," he explains.

The head has three horns, and the way it moves almost makes it look like a Chinese dragon that could fly, as seen in many movies. It's lime green with a little orange mouth. Stephen hands the little creature to me so that I can pass it along to others after my turn. Terrified yet determined, the bug is placed on my hand. It feels so soft and fragile. Its skin is freezing even though it's hot out. It enjoys the warmth of my hand. *How cute.* I rub its body, surprisingly unafraid at this point, then pass it on to the tourist next to me.

Wow. What a huge accomplishment. I never thought I'd be able to willingly pet one. On the tree, many dragon caterpillars squirm around, searching for leaves to eat or maybe a place to start a cocoon. A black and orange butterfly comes out of nowhere.

"See that butterfly? That's the evolved form," Pablo says, marveling at the sight.

Apparently, this species is very rare. They are from Europe and Asia but made their way here somehow.

I hold onto Stephen's hand—not just to keep from falling again, but because it's warm, and because he's so loving. Making it to the bottom, we are both completely gasping for air. I could see from a distance that the boat where we first came in from is still there with the driver waiting. Torches get lit near the boat, along with a table set up with dinner and many bottles of water. I was so nervous being this close to Stephen the whole time that I forgot about being hungry. Familiar slow classics are playing in the background using an extremely ancient battery-powered radio. After eating chicken and rice, Stephen asks me to dance. He doesn't exactly say it, but the way he holds out his hand to take mine and looks toward the radio, I already know what he means.

Pablo brings out his maracas to go along with the slow beat. Other couples join in, thank goodness. Being the center of attention would put too much pressure on us. I go with the flow of mostly hugging and moving left and right. Being in his arms feels like being in heaven. I want to kiss his cute, dark eyebrows. Instead, I put my face in his chest, wishing the moment would last forever. The music in Brazil is peaceful and loving.

Stephen kisses my forehead and whispers into my ear, "Eve, por favor não va."

I'm not a hundred percent sure what that means. But to me, it sounds like, "Please don't go."

Today is my last day. This is too sad. I've gotten to see so much and am so proud of myself. Holding and petting a bug while not feeling any fear was one of my biggest accomplishments. Also, feeling confident in myself was a huge change of pace that could be implemented in my personal life. But then I met this hunk of a man. In my eyes, he's the most gorgeous, kindest person I've ever encountered. He respects my boundaries and makes me feel like the most beautiful woman in the world. How could I even respond to those big brown eyes right now? I melt.

The night gets much darker, and we hear strange sounds in the distance. The tour guide tries to scare people by telling them that the caymans tend to do their hunting during the night. The driver takes accountability for everyone, and we head back to the cruise. I say goodnight to everyone and head to my room to shower. I can barely breathe. My mind is too busy spiraling with the beautiful moments from this past week. My heart can't comprehend my own feelings. I want to sneak into Stephen's room and cuddle the rest of the night. Unfortunately, the walls are paper-thin. Pablo might hear, and I don't want to get Stephen into any more trouble. I'm able to hear the neighbor in the other room snoring. In the room to the right, a man sings beautifully while playing guitar. The perfect sound to fall asleep to...

CHAPTER 32

A beautiful man stands before me now. His face is as clear as a polished mirror; it's Stephen. He gently touches my face with the back of his hand, kissing my forehead softly, sending a warm shiver down my spine. The moonlight bathes us in a glowing embrace, illuminating his features with a pearlescent sheen. Toucans chirp in the distance, enhancing the magic of the moment. I lean in, yearning to savor the sweetness of his lips, when suddenly, a loud bang shatters the tranquility. My world jolts violently as my eyes snap open, pulled back from the dream into stark reality that I'm late for breakfast.

The other tourists run down the hallways loudly. *Ugh, my dream was just getting good.* Today, my flight will arrive, taking me away from my dream home. I come out of the room, furious yet flustered at the thought of that kiss. Brushing my teeth or washing my face doesn't occur to me. I probably look like a bedhead; oh well, there shouldn't be anyone here right now since they all left on the next excursion. At this rate, my flight could leave me behind, and it wouldn't be entirely a bad thing. I wouldn't mind staying an extra week, maybe a month. Actually, forever sounds better.

The chef recommends a vegetable omelet paired with a perfect cup of coffee that can only be found in Brazil. Thank goodness there's no one in sight. It saves me from the embarrassment of someone witnessing my pajamas. I resort to wearing mismatched socks with a huge hole at the bottom after being out of clean clothes for many days.

"Good morning, Evelyn," says Stephen, walking towards me.

Oh no, I spoke too soon, as usual. Is it too late to run? How embarrassing. *Crap.* How do I explain? No one was supposed to be here this morning.

"Uh, sorry, I just woke up." I apologize.

"Beautiful," he says with those loving, deep brown eyes.

My heart melts. Apologizing for the way I look isn't needed. Stephen grabs some breakfast and takes it back to his room. Had I known that was an option, I would have done it from day one. The whole time, I wanted to be respectful by letting them serve me breakfast as they insisted on giving me the best seat closest to the food. It is one of those grab-and-sit-down types of buffets.

I'm going to miss having someone cook for me every day. If it were up to me, I would have starved by now, living alone. Mom often invites me over for dinner, even though my papa gets mad that he can't be in his underwear all the time. That is the beauty of being retired with no more children living there. You can do anything you want at home.

My meal gets cut short as I remember that I haven't had any time to pack. *Oops.* How could I even be worried? I can't stop thinking about my dream. I've never craved kissing someone this bad. I wouldn't even know what in the world to do. How does my mouth need to move? And the tongue? *Gross.* Hopefully, whoever kisses me guides me through the process first, before a huge mistake is made. But hey, a lady can still dream about what it would be like. In my mind, lips are warm and very soft. There has to be some kind of power that's produced when it's touched by someone else, almost like a ticklish feeling with unquenching pleasure involved.

Disappearing back to my room, I fold all my clothes neatly and throw all the dirty, stinky ones into a plastic bag. It smells musty, like sweat and dirty water. My laundry machine is going to hate me when I get back. Toiletries aren't a problem since the places I've gone to have offered them. My wavy hair is as soft as ever. Using natural water with no chlorine makes a huge difference. Even the products don't have any harmful effects here. The smell isn't too bad either.

I decide to call Sarah; I miss her wisdom. It's been over a week since I've heard her voice, not because of connection issues but because I've been extremely busy all these days. I wanted to make the most out of this trip.

"Hey, Sarah, I miss your voice!" I say. Thank goodness she answered after two rings. It's not easy being on a time crunch.

"Eve! It's been so boring without you around. I miss you! How are things?" she says, amused that I finally called.

"Things are, well, amazing. I met someone." I should have kept this for a much later conversation, but at this point, I really need some advice.

"Say whaaaaaaaaaaaaaaaat? Please tell me everything!"

I tell her all about Stephen. The loving embrace. The sensual dance and respect he has for me as a person. The language barrier. The feelings I have for him. The request for me to stay.

"So, what do you think I should do? I really don't want to leave, not ever."

"Well, you need to pray about this first. If you stay, you might be rushing into decisions instead of thinking them through. You also have to consider logistics. Without a proper visa, you really can't stay permanently," she continues. "However, if you truly like this guy, go for it. If there is a will, there is always a way. Spend the rest of the time you can with him. Somehow, communicate your feelings before your flight."

"Oh shoot! I've got one hour before I need to head to the airport."

"Go get 'em, girl."

"Talk to you later. Love you, I mean it, bye!"

I hang up, get my bags ready, and finish off by getting the room fixed up. My mom taught me to never leave things messy. No one's my maid. If I mess it up in any way, I must be the one to fix it. Fixing the white puffy sheets while looking out the beautiful windows towards the Amazon River, I feel like crying. I don't want to leave.

Okay. I'm going to do this. It's now or never. This moment can slip away forever, go completely wrong, or go exactly the way I want it to. What's there to lose? The courage to knock on Stephen's door comes out of nowhere. He takes his time to open it, but once it happens, welp, he is shirtless. Embarrassed, he hides behind the door frame and lets out a yelp as if he expected someone else. Probably his father.

"Eve, are you ready to go?" Stephen plays it cool. "One second."

He returns with a very manly tank top, exposing his nice upper arms. I try my best not to stare, but it's impossible not to. Oh right. I should probably explain what I'm doing here with only a few minutes before we need to go to the mainland and catch a ride to the airport.

"Listen, Stephen, I truly want to say, er." Instant redness and choking on words start to occur. *I can do this!* If it is not released, the feelings will be hidden for the rest of my life. I don't want to live with more regrets. "The truth is, er, I can't live this life without you."

His mouth drops. I hope that my words came out clearly enough to be understood. One of the other guests barrels down the hallway, shoving everything in his path aside with little regard. An expensive vase shatters, but the man doesn't stop to fix his mistake.

"Sorry, excuse me!!!" he bellows, his voice echoing off the walls as if he's about to burst with urgency. His frantic movements create a whirlwind of chaos as he heads in my direction, not giving any indication of stopping. Stephen grabs my arm, pulling me inside his room, saving me from being pummeled by the very large man. His room is a little smaller than the one I stayed in. But why? Maybe since he works as an assistant tour guide. I wonder if there's anyone else in his life. The job entails meeting a lot of different people from all over the world. But no way. I decide no one can have him. He is mine.

Instead of embarrassing myself with words that I don't really know how to express, I grab Stephen slowly and cautiously, kissing his cheeks with tears in my eyes. We dance back and forth with no music but the song from last night playing inside my head. He massages my shoulders and arms with his vibrant touch. I kiss his neck as he makes his way down to my hips with his hands. Stopping himself from going any further, he kisses my forehead when a tear lands on me.

A random idea pops into my brain of writing my mailing address and email on a napkin. Maybe we can write to each other until I can return to his arms? But what if he moves on? Oh well, there's no point in pondering these things right now. It's already sad enough. Sarah made a strong point: If it's meant to be, it will be. Language barrier or not.

The time is here. Pablo, Stephen, and I embark on the boat, a two-hour trip spent in utter silence, holding Stephen's hand tightly. Pablo does notice, but he doesn't say a word. Saying goodbye to Stephen opens a brand-new deep pit inside my heart. Pablo gives me a massive bear hug, sad to see me go.

"Please take good care of yourself. Next time, you can stay at our house for free the entire time. We'd love to have you again," Pablo suggests.

"I'd like that. Thank you so much for everything. It was truly magical." A tear drips down my face.

Stephen pulls me in for our final goodbye and kisses my cheek. Sneaky. I love it. I'm sure once I go, he'll have to explain what exactly happened between us to his family. I owe an explanation to Sarah when I get back, too. The story is too special. I'll keep some things to myself, of course. It's mine to ponder for the rest of my life.

I wave one last goodbye. It's too hard for me. Tears gush down my face, not allowing me to move. I turn toward them to get one last look and see Stephen frowning with a depressed look on his face. Maybe I shouldn't go. But it's too late; TSA pressures me for my ID, passport, and airline ticket, forcing me to move past the checkpoint.

CHAPTER 33

$\mathcal{F}$eelings of regret already kick in, but then Sarah's advice pops into my consciousness. Stephen has my contact information; he'll write if he really wants to. Even though there isn't a traditional mailing system in Brazil, as there is in the U.S., there are companies that ship products out. It is in God's hands. It's time to go home.

It feels odd not to have someone watching over me. No safety net anywhere in sight. I miss him even though it's been only five minutes since I got to the gate. Hunger was dismissed the moment he kissed my cheeks. Emotions don't allow for a normal eating schedule. Why does it have to hurt so much?

My boarding group gets called. Normally, I'd be the first to get up to get the first dibs at taking a seat. Not today. Sluggishly and lazily, I rise slowly to the very back of the line, hoping that there will magically be no more space left on the plane. Sometimes airlines do overbook flights. I notice people with tons of luggage. Pablo and Stephen wouldn't have left the airport yet. Knowing them, they'll probably wait another hour to make sure my plane takes off. It's the kind of people they are, always looking out for others. Maybe there is still some hope of staying. Who am I kidding? Everyone goes straight to their seat. It's a nice and spacious airplane.

Crying myself to sleep has become one of my talents over the last few years. It should be easy to do since I'm starving and plan to refuse any food offered to me. Time on the plane will feel like two seconds. The person next to me probably feels uncomfortable since I'm super emotional right now, and tons of snot is coming out of my nose. Anxiety hits my chest like a whirlwind. It's an indication that it's time to settle down before my eyelids start getting stress bubbles. My doctor says that once they have developed, they do come back periodically through stress-induced triggers. Eyedrops are my best friend during these times. The pharmacy sells all kinds of different types, such as mint, regular, and soothing red eyes.

The pilot finally prompts everyone to unfasten their seat-belts, and I bolt to the bathroom. Sadly, other people have the same exact idea, making the line nearly impossible. I take a deep breath, deciding that holding it in is currently the best option until they open the airplane doors. While the seats at the back are the most affordable, they also mean an extra thirty minutes when it's time to get off the plane.

I get to baggage claim, exhausted from the flight and the last few weeks. Someone pokes my shoulder. Without thinking, I turn around to see my four greatest friends in the flesh, along with my loving parents. I've missed them so much. It has been about three weeks since I left. I planned on getting an Uber home, but luckily, they saved me a forty-dollar ride. They give me a million hugs and ask invasive questions. My papa drives us to their house, where there is a surprise dinner waiting for me. Mom made my favorite meal, arroz con pollo, which is chicken with rice—Cuban style. We share a meal as a big, happy family. I love them all so much. I am blessed to have them in my life.

"Mija, tell us everything," Mom urges me.

And so the stories begin.

~

I THROW my bags to the corner of the room, feeling overwhelmed by the stories I spit out. The mess in the apartment makes it clear that I didn't get to clean before leaving. *How embarrassing.* I must have been in a hurry that morning. There's such a good feeling sleeping in the bed that has been mine since my teenage years. It was passed on to me from my parents, who didn't know what to do with it after I moved out. They bought it for me as I started growing taller. I never once thought to buy another mattress since they're overpriced. Living in an apartment for this long was not part of the plan. Initially, it was going to be for one year, enough time to save up for a house. That's when I found out that many banks do not give out loans to those with zero or low credit scores.

The next day, Lucas and I make plans to meet at the beach to talk things over. I need to get all this baggage out of me before I blow up. The beach is one of the places where I can unwind and be myself. Pleased with that, he says yes immediately, probably thinking that I will accept his feelings even though they make absolutely no sense to me. Sarah helped with getting his phone number at work. She didn't want to have to ask him for it. Instead, she found it in the employee contact information database.

Nervous beyond measure, I park the car. I am ready to face him like the strong woman that I am. There is no easier way of doing this, but it has to be done. I want to move on with my life.

"Lucas, I had a lot of time to think. Reflection was one of the biggest goals of my trip, along with conquering my fear of bugs," I continue. "You've hurt me. More than anyone else in this world. Some days, I feel lower than a worm deep in the ground. I hated myself for many years. Even now, it's hard to accept everything that has happened." Tears of anger rush down, attempting to stop my words from flowing out. *Come on, Eve, you can do this!*

"Eve, I…" Lucas, being Lucas, already tries to interrupt.

"Hush, please, let me continue."

"Go ahead, sorry."

"You have harassed me. Took the position I clearly deserved. Made others hate me for no apparent reason. Pushed me against lockers. Threatened me with harmful insects. It's sickening."

"Eve, the truth is, my parents were never there for me. My dad left my mom for another woman because he never wanted me. The ultimatum was to get an abortion or else she'd end up raising me alone." Lucas goes on, "My mom became severely depressed, resorted to drugs, and beat me on multiple occasions. My life hasn't been easy."

"I understand that you had a hard childhood; I get it. But that is not an excuse to take it out on me. I will forgive you only because I personally need to let this grudge go. It is literally killing me. But you have to promise me something."

"Yes, anything."

"Stop hurting people."

Lucas agrees with tears in his eyes, promising to learn how to be a better person. He comes in close to offer a hug, but I reject it instantly. It feels so good to stand up for myself. A backbone that somehow developed after nights of crying and trying to let the anger go. It isn't easy to forgive. But after seeing different cultures and the way people are treated in other countries, I made up my mind that this is not the way to live. There are bigger things out there. Greater purposes in life are calling my name, waiting for me to have the courage to say yes. Becoming stagnant in life is a newly awakened fear of mine.

Being around Lucas without resentment becomes a lot easier. We see each other a few times with my friends around. Through therapy, Lucas begins to change, becoming more pleasant to be around. Some of the friends he once harassed back in elementary school have since forgiven him.

Making peace with insects was the best thing I could have ever done. They fly near me now, and it doesn't faze me as much. I remember what Rudy told me: to deeply respect them. Bugs don't pose nearly as much of a threat as staying in the same spot forever with unfulfilled dreams. Work will always be there. The ability to make more money will always be there. Endless opportunities will not be. Aging takes away the freedom of traveling. When sickness arrives at my doorstep, there is no way to avoid it, even if my doctor tells me a million times to continue taking my vitamins every day. More than anything else, I want to find my purpose in life. To find the kind of love that would never leave me lonely again.

EPILOGUE

There he is, standing before me. The beautiful face I've waited two years to see. His hair looks dark and luscious, a beautiful curly style that could only be achieved with natural water and zero product use. That smile that melted my heart so long ago still has the same exact effect.

Wind swishes my hair all around as I walk towards him. My armpits flood with sweat, but there's no time to think about antiperspirants. His arms wrap around me for a warm embrace. Our lips press together as he moves them with a slow flow to match my rhythm. I clearly have no valid experience. Warm saliva ends up dripping down my face, and I can feel my heart beating faster than ever.

"Hey, Eve!" Pablo interrupts our reunion. *Typical.* Stephen steps back, showing respect to his father. I look over to see Stephen with flushed, pink cheeks.

"Pablo! I missed you guys so much! I'm ecstatic to be here. Thank you so much for having me," I say with deep appreciation.

"The pleasure is all mine. Come on over. There are many people here to see you."

Preparations took forever since all my personal belongings had to be sold. Convincing my family and friends to agree with my plan also became a big stumbling block. One way or another, it's my life. People had their opinions and tried to convince me not to do it because too many risks were involved. It was now or never. I decided that going to college was never for me.

Thinking about getting a traditional job made me depressed. It wasn't what I wanted to do in life. My love for dancing heightened after my trips, enabling me to find a greater purpose. With the money I had left over from the trip, I opened up a dance studio where I taught all ages how to express themselves through the art of dance. I paid my overdue rent and made it to the end of the leasing contract.

A few months after my trip, a letter came in the mail. It was all beat up and crumbled, but the moment I opened it, my face went numb. To my surprise, it was Stephen writing to me in Portuguese. I paid a translator to help me understand what was written. Stephen wondered how I had been doing after my journey came to an end. We wrote back and forth to each other on a monthly basis. I even started learning Portuguese using free YouTube videos and apps. Fluency was nowhere near perfect, but it was good enough to continue writing to him without spending an arm and a leg to get it translated.

Stephen finally popped a suggestion after we kept complaining about our lives being so lonely without each other, and that long-distance relationships didn't always work out. At least, that's what I've heard from family, friends, and movies. I'd yearned to be in his arms.

"Come to Brazil. Live with me," he wrote in one of the letters. He had been practicing English with his father.

I never truly thought about making such a huge move before. Unhappiness with my life has been going on for many years. Even after reconciling with Lucas, I still felt something was missing. The logistics of everything were very stressful to think about, but traveling on a budget is always possible with a bit of dedication and hard work. Becoming a dance teacher helped me get through the days. I now had something to live for instead of being stuck inside my apartment, contemplating life. While I waited to save enough money to fund my dream, Stephen and I continued sending letters back and forth, making plans. He and his father, Pablo, started a project of building us a small hut to live in.

Communication was still quite difficult since his English wasn't too good, but I promised myself that once I got there, I'd teach him everything that I knew. The first picture I received of the hut looked like it had been taken with one of those disposable cameras from back in the '90s. All that aside, the hut was coming along beautifully. The roof was made from dried palm leaves. To think that soon this beautiful place was going to be mine. No more paying rent to an angry landlord or struggling to pay bills on time.

It all felt like a dream.

Now, Stephen grabs me from behind, hugging me and placing his face on my neck. It tickles, but feels so good at the same time. Still silent, he walks me over to our new home, the hut. It had been completed without him telling me. The front porch is made from bamboo. It feels so sturdy. The door is wide open, welcoming me home.

Suddenly, we come to a halt at the door frame. Stephen's intense gaze pierces through to my very soul as he lowers himself onto one knee, the world around us fading into a blur. With a deliberate motion, he unveils a small velvet box, holding it out towards me. As he opens it, the soft glint of a ring catches my eye–a masterpiece adorned with delicate gold, shimmering silver, and warm rose gold, all intricately set with stunning diamonds that dance with light.

Oh my goodness! Is this really happening?

The ring bears the marks of history, its surface caked with small dings and scratches that tell a story of time and love. Each imperfection whispers of the hands that once wore it, suggesting at least two or three generations have cherished it before this day. There's an undeniable beauty in its character, and it fills me with a sense of being connected. It's going to be mine forever.

"Eve, will you spend the rest of your life with me?" Stephen says lovingly and very sexily. I burst out crying. I never thought anyone could love me. From the corner of my eye, I see the entire village gathering together outside the hut, waiting for my response.

"Stephen, I've come all this way." I gasp for air. "All I have ever wanted is you."

It's enough of a yes—and everyone floods us with hugs, love, and warmth. It's more than I've ever dreamed of.

The End

ACKNOWLEDGMENTS

Woohoo! You've made it to the end of the book! Pat yourself on the back because that was indeed a wild ride. I want to thank you for taking the time to buy, read, understand, and love this story. I cannot wait to eventually meet you in person at a convention, book fair, art gallery, or even on social media. If you enjoyed this book, please bring the biggest smile to my face by leaving a review on Amazon and Goodreads. Feedback is one of the greatest gifts because it helps me improve as a writer and as a person in general.

I want to thank my amazing, perfect, loving husband, Mark, who made all of this possible. You're the best thing in my life and my greatest coach. Year after year, you encourage me to grow and be the best person I can possibly be. Your love has brightened my life, making all my dreams come true. I can't wait to experience what the rest of our lives together will be like. I'm so happy that I walk in love with you each and every day. I get to wake up to the love of my life—my best friend.

Thank you to Jesus Christ, my Lord and Savior, for putting all these ideas in my heart. In the middle of the night, I get more and more ideas. I would never have thought that I could actually become a published author without prayer and guidance. Multiple nights I spent crying, wondering if I made the right choice leaving my job—you comforted me through it all, letting me know that you have a bigger plan for my life.

Serra, you are literally the best and most motivational friend I've ever had in my life. I'm so glad that I met you at church, even though we both cried multiple times during the service because of shame. I feel that we share a lot of the same dreams. I'm excited to continue growing with you as we both become full-fledged artists and authors.

To my sister, Priscilla, aka "Monk-ey," thank you so much for being here for me even when you are extremely busy saving lives as a nurse. You always think of me even when life gets difficult. Thank you, Aaliyah, "Bob", my beautiful, precious niece, for your support and love, especially on social media when I feel that no one cares about my posts—you always do. I love you both, sis and little sis.

Pat, little bro, I'm grateful that you always check up on me midweek when I need it the most. Thank you for always asking me how my book is going and being genuinely interested in my work. To my parents and Abuela, thank you so much for giving me a taste of Cuban culture, although sometimes I feel that I don't belong, you still make it work for me with so much love.

Nanay Nazaria, thank you for always loving us so deeply. You paved the way, showing us all what a kindhearted, humble person should be like. Loving your family well was your highest priority. I will see you in heaven someday. I love you so much.

To my editor, Leilani, you did such an amazing job. When you sent me back the first set of edits, my mouth literally dropped. I could not believe the amount of detail you put into it and the care for every single word. Thank you so much for loving my story and nurturing it just as much as I did. You are truly a one-of-a-kind person.

To my fabulous artist, Emiliano, I am so happy with the book cover you created out of just a few words from my vision. You, sir, are extremely gifted with talent brought from God himself. Evelyn looks so beautiful—exactly the way I envisioned her as I was writing. Thank you so much for everything. I was seriously crying when you sent me the initial sketches. I couldn't believe that someone could get the art that spot on.

62641349R00125

ABOUT THE AUTHOR

Victoria Loria is a writer with a massive ambition. Nothing can stop her from pouring out what's on that big heart and soul. She has a passion for displaying her faith within her writing, along with vivid descriptions of real-life experiences. She is a military veteran, a middle child (ugly duckling), a madly in-love wife, and a sucker for romance/adventure.

CONNECT ONLINE
VictoriaLoriaRawrt.com
@VictoriaLoriaRawrt